SPARK

(Electric Series #2)

E. L. TODD

Fallen Publishing

Spark

Editing Services provided by Final-Edits.com

Chapter One

Volt

I walked into the bar and felt the dull ache return. My heart was constantly vulnerable, on the edge of catching fire and burning out. Taylor was always in my thoughts, and she was always in my dreams. I wanted this woman— and I was afraid I wouldn't get her.

I spotted her talking to Natalie in the corner. She wore a skin-tight purple dress that hugged her beautiful hips and showed off her ridiculously sexy legs. Her hair was pulled back into a sexy updo, and I could only assume that was because the dress was backless.

Oh man.

While she looked great with her new fashion taste, I actually preferred her older stuff. I loved the big dresses with strange colors. I loved the globe earrings and the snake ring she wore from time to time. I loved her strange and quirky self—because she was perfect the way she was.

After I grabbed a drink, I joined their conversation. My eyes were preoccupied with Taylor, and I hardly glanced at Natalie. Everyone else in the room seemed insignificant next to the woman I'd fallen for. I still couldn't wrap my mind around the truth.

That I'd fallen for someone at all.

Natalie waved her hand in front of my face. "Uh, hi?"

Shit, was I making it obvious? "Hey, Nat. How are you?"

"Wasn't sure if you even noticed me..." She was dressed in her finest as well, but I didn't pay enough attention to know what color her dress was or how her hair was done. Everyone else in the room turned into strange blurs and shapes.

"Of course I did. You look nice." My eyes examined Taylor's shoulder, noticing the small freckles on her skin. I'd never noticed them before, and now I wanted to kiss each one—forever.

"Still haven't looked at me..."

Now I was just irritated. I turned to her and gave her my coldest stare. "Happy now?"

Natalie rolled her eyes and walked away.

Thank god she was gone.

"Don't mind her," Taylor said. "She's just a little moody right now."

The second she left my sight, I stopped thinking about her. All I cared about was Taylor and the way her hair was pulled off her neck. Her delicate skin was revealed, and I got a hard-on in my jeans when I thought about kissing her everywhere. "I like the thing you've done with your hair…" I pointed at her neck like there would be any misunderstanding of what I was talking about.

"Uh, thanks." She absentmindedly touched it.

I cleared my throat then masked my unease with a drink. I acted like a total loser who had absolutely no game. Taylor would never notice me at this rate.

"I was too lazy to do my hair so I just threw it up—"

"I think it looks amazing."

She was just about to take a drink but faltered at my outburst. "Well…thanks."

I was just making this worse and worse. Why couldn't I just turn on the charm like I did with all the other women? Why was this so difficult? She was my best friend, so I should know exactly what to say.

Except I was clueless.

"Do you have plans this weekend?" I suspected she was doing something with that piece-of-shit loser.

"Sage is visiting his parents on Saturday, so we're going to go out on Sunday." Her eyes lit up slightly when she mentioned him.

I hated him.

3

Loathed him.

"So…is this getting serious?" If she loved the guy, then I couldn't intervene, but they just met and Taylor wouldn't jump into something that quickly. She had a good head on her shoulders.

"We've only been out a few times, but I have a really good feeling about him. I think my search for Mr. Right is over."

Ouch.

Fuck.

No.

"Don't rush into anything. Remember, you really don't know him."

"That's true," she said. "But I just have a hunch. The chemistry was there the moment we met. And we met under such strange circumstances that it makes me wonder if it was meant to be or something…"

I felt sick.

"I sound like a crazy person, don't I?" She looked into her glass.

"No…not at all."

"I'm not obsessed with marriage."

"I never said you were."

4

"I just want a partner I can spend my life with, have kids with, and I think he might be it."

"You don't know him well enough to say that." How could I have a fair chance if she was already making all these assumptions when she hardly knew him?

"You're right. I don't know him well enough. But...I still have a good feeling about it."

I hated myself even more. She was right under my nose for the past six months, and I could have had her whenever I wanted her. All I had to do was ask her out and she would have been mine. But no, I chose to be a goddamn idiot instead.

She stared at me, and I didn't even notice. "Volt, are you alright?"

"Yeah." I cleared my throat. "I just think I might be coming down with something."

"Oh no. And you just had the stomach flu not too long ago."

"I did?" *When did that happen?*

"Yeah. A few weeks ago..."

Now I remembered. I was using it as an excuse to avoid her. "Oh yeah. You're right."

Taylor grew suspicious, and I didn't blame her. "Are you sure you're all right?"

Other than losing the one woman I couldn't live without? Fabulous. "Yeah. I'm sure. If you're free on Saturday, want to get dinner?"

"Sure. I'd love that."

"Where do you want to go?"

A playful smile formed on her lips.

"Pita Paradise?" I asked with a laugh.

"What? It's good."

"There are so many amazing restaurants in the city and that's what you want? Tayz, it's not even that good."

"I'm a weirdo. I know."

"I didn't say you were a weirdo. You just have interesting taste."

She shrugged. "What can I say? I'm a little quirky."

"But I love you that way." I never meant anything more in my life. The words left my lips, and I realized just how deep I was in. The moment I couldn't have her was the moment I knew how I truly felt. A shooting star had crossed my path, but I didn't take the time to look at it and appreciate it. By the time I understood how rare and beautiful it was, it already passed.

And I missed my chance.

***

After dinner at Pita Paradise, we went to a piano bar. The place was crowded with people but the conversation volume was low. Everyone was dressed classy, wearing dresses and heels, and the men wore collared shirts. I didn't usually wear a button up unless I was working, but tonight I did.

And I knew why.

Taylor was on her third drink, and she was laughing for no reason at all. "That one episode of *South Park*...Kenny dies." She slapped the table as she relived whatever episode she was thinking of. "Oh man. Good stuff."

I didn't get the joke, but I loved watching her laugh. Her eyes had an adventurous glow and her smile was to die for.

I wish I were the one who made her laugh.

She was almost finished with her third drink and she probably shouldn't have another one. "So...how many women did you pick up this week?"

My sexual appetite had disappeared when I realized how I felt about Taylor. I wasn't in a relationship with her and she didn't even know how I felt, but I couldn't be with anyone else. And I didn't want to be. "None."

"None?" She laughed like she thought I was making a joke. "Come on, be serious."

"I am being serious."

She laughed again, having no idea what she was laughing at. "Yeah right. I can't even imagine that. Your head would explode if you weren't getting laid on a daily basis."

"Not really." I was too depressed to feel anything.

"Then you must be watching a ton of porn. Like, a ton."

I wasn't doing that either. "No."

She grabbed another drink from the bartender and took a drink so big she almost spilled it down her dress. "Shh… I have a secret."

"Yeah?" That was her last drink. I wasn't letting her have another.

"Come here." She waved me toward her.

Getting close to her made me nervous. There was no way I could have my lips near hers and not kiss her.

She grabbed my hand and pulled me closer. Without realizing it, she pulled my hand right against her chest. I could feel the swell of her boob.

And it was nice.

Since she didn't know what was going on, I pulled my hand away.

But she yanked it back. "You want to know my secret?"

We were close enough for a kiss.

I should just go for it.

I could lie and say I was drunk.

We'd have a great kiss and go home together. She would have such amazing sex she wouldn't think about that loser she was dating. She would be mine and we could start something new.

But that would make me an asshole. "What's your secret?"

She chuckled before she pressed her lips directly against my ear.

My spine shivered when I felt her lips brush past my skin. Her breath amplified in my eardrum, and I could feel my dick harden at record speed.

"I watch porn." She chuckled and pulled away.

I looked at her and grinned from ear to ear. "Really?" This was a topic I needed to know more about.

"I know. I'm nasty." She laughed again.

"What are you into?"

Her cheeks blushed. "Stuff..."

"Come on, tell me."

"I don't know. What are you into?"

My taste had changed recently. "A beautiful brunette who's a high school teacher."

A puzzled look formed on her face. "What?"

She was too drunk to understand anything. "Nevermind. Now tell me what you like."

"All sorts of things...even threesomes."

"Say what?" I asked with a laugh.

"Since you said you do threesomes a lot, I thought I would see what the fuss is about."

"And?"

"It's pretty hot."

"With two guys?"

"No. Two girls."

Even hotter. "Yeah?"

"I think it's sexy when a man can please two women."

Then I was her man. "If you weren't so drunk right now, I'd make a move."

She laughed like she thought I was joking.

I wasn't.

She finished her drink then tried to order another.

"Nope. I'm cutting you off."

She pouted her lips like a whiny kid. "Why?"

"I've never seen you this drunk." I sipped her drink. "Damn, no wonder why you're wasted. They're putting some serious shit in here."

She chuckled.

"Let's get you home."

"But we're having fun."

"Show me your favorite porn when we get to your place."

"What?" she asked incredulously. "That's just weird." She tried to get off the stool but slipped.

I grabbed her by the waist and righted her. "Be careful, Bambi."

"I'm not a deer. I only have three legs..."

My eyebrow rose. "Three?"

"Yeah." She counted each leg. "One...two..." Then she stopped with a puzzled look on her face. "That's weird. I could have sworn I had three."

I didn't laugh at her even though I wanted to. "It's definitely time to get you home."

She took a step forward but her heel slipped on the tile.

She was definitely Bambi. I scooped her up into my arms and held her against my chest. "I'll give you a lift."

She wrapped her arms around my neck. "Geez, it's high up here. You ever get scared?"

"You get used to it." I carried her out of the bar and up the sidewalk. I'd never held her before, and I loved how light she was in my arms. Our bodies were made specifically to form to each other. Was I the only one who noticed that?

She set her clutch in her lap then leaned her head on my shoulder, not caring about all the people staring at us as we walked by. She closed her eyes and seemed to have fallen into a somber state from all the alcohol.

My apartment was closer than hers. "You want to go to my place?" My offer wasn't totally selfless. Okay, it wasn't selfless at all.

"Yeah...I'm tired."

Yes.

***

I set her down on my bed and pulled off her heels. "At first, I thought you were a light weight, but now that I know they put bombs of liquor in your drink, I'm surprised you lasted so long."

She laid her head on my pillow. "I love liquor."

I chuckled then pulled the covers back so I could tuck her in.

She sat up and unzipped the back of her dress.

I froze as I waited for whatever she was about to do.

She pulled the dress loose from her body then tossed it on the floor. She only wore a strapless black bra, and her tits were pushed together in the fabric. A cleavage line formed, and the silver chain around her neck contrasted against the color of her skin.

I just stared, infatuated.

She pulled her hair out of her face then grabbed the sheets.

I couldn't stop staring.

She was nearly naked in my bed. Her bare skin was touching the mattress I slept on every night. Her natural

13

scent would stick to my blankets and infuse the fabric for weeks.

I couldn't comprehend what was happening.

I opened my nightstand and pulled out one of my t-shirts and tossed it to her. "Maybe you'll be more comfortable in this." *And I'll be able to control myself while I lay beside you.*

She didn't sit up to grab it because she was too tired. She felt around on the blanket until she found it. Then, she pulled it on quickly, yanking it over her body and getting comfortable. Once she was adjusted, she lay back down.

The gentlemanly thing to do was sleep on the couch in the living room. I didn't mind giving her the bed because I'd never make a woman sleep anywhere else, but I didn't want to be in a different room.

I wanted to sleep beside her.

I pulled off my shirt and jeans then grabbed my sweatpants from a drawer. Despite my strong urge to lay right beside her in bed, I managed to convince myself to head into the living room.

"Where are you going?" She sat up when she heard my footsteps recede. Her mascara started to smear, and her shirt was several sizes too big. Who knew a woman could look so sexy in baggy clothes.

"Sleeping on the couch." I stood in the doorway and waited for her to invite me back to bed. Actually, I *hoped* she would invite me back to bed. My body could keep her warm all night long, and her heart could chase away my ghosts.

"No. Sleep in here." She pulled the covers back so I could slip inside.

I knew she was drunk and confused, but I wasn't going to deny the offer. She'd slept with me before, so I used it as an excuse to hop in. I slid in between the sheets and lay beside her in the dark.

There were a few inches of space between us, but those inches felt like miles. Her quiet breathing filled the room, and I could hear her small chest rise and fall with every breath she took. She kicked her feet a few times as she tried to get comfortable.

I lay still and stared at the ceiling.

She turned around then moved into my side within a heartbeat. It happened so quickly I had no time to prepare for it. Her arm hugged my waist and she rested her face on my arm. Her slender legs settled against mine. She even tucked one leg between my thighs.

This was heaven.

I moved my arm under her head and pulled her even closer to me. Her head moved to my shoulder and her light breathing fell on my neck. Her hand rested on my flat stomach, and I loved feeling her weightless fingers there.

It felt so good I wanted to growl.

When women spent the night, they usually stuck to their side of the bed and I stuck to mine. I wasn't a fan of cuddling. It was nothing against my partners. I was just too hot to be comfortable next to another body.

But with Taylor, I couldn't get enough.

I wanted to roll her onto her back and kiss her aggressively. Her nails would run down my back, leaving marks that would linger for days. She would moan for me, asking for more. And she would kiss me like she loved me.

I knew that fantasy would come true if I made a move. If I kissed her and made love to her, she would want it as much as I did. The next morning, we'd have to talk about it, and that would be the perfect opportunity to ask her out on a date—and ask her to be mine.

But that would be a fucked up thing to do.

She was drunk. Drunk enough that she took off her dress right in front of me. It didn't matter how good of friends we were. She never would have done that if she were sober.

I couldn't do it.

I wanted her to be mine, and I was willing to play dirty to make that happen, but I wasn't willing to take advantage of her to achieve it—even if I had the best intentions.

Because above all else, I was her friend.

And friends didn't do that to each other.

She released a quiet sigh just before she fell asleep. Her hold on me loosened and she drifted off into her dreams.

I had a moment of weakness and did something I shouldn't. I turned into her and placed a soft kiss right on her lips. It felt just as good as the last time we had an embrace. My lips were so hot they felt cold, and my entire body came alive with ecstasy.

I could have sworn she kissed me back, just a little. Her lips moved with mine slightly, and when I pulled away, they were slightly open. Maybe it was just my imagination, but I could have sworn it happened.

She released another sigh, telling me she drifted back to whatever dream she was having.

Chapter Two

Taylor

I woke up with a massive migraine.

The worst one ever.

It was even worse than the one I had after my college graduation.

It was that bad.

The second I opened my eyes, the throbbing became worse. It was dark in the bedroom because the shades were shut, but that was still too bright for me. I saw the dark nightstand and the baseball bat in the corner.

I didn't own a baseball bat.

Wait, where was I?

I sat up and realized I was in Volt's bed. We must have crashed here after the bar we went to. I couldn't remember much of it, but I did recall Volt carrying me somewhere.

"Hey, baby." Volt sat at the edge of the bed and held out his open palm. Two painkillers sat in the center.

I snatched them out of his hand and swallowed them dry. "Oh, thank god."

Then he handed me a beer.

"You actually expect me to drink that?"

"You think it's for me?"

"I just took meds. You aren't supposed to drink alcohol."

"It'll be fine." He pressed it on me. "The best way to cure a hangover is to keep drinking."

"What?"

"I know it sounds crazy but it's true."

I took the bottle and drank half of it.

"There's my girl." He rubbed my back gently.

I set the bottle on the nightstand with a loud clunk and just wanted to go back to sleep. I hadn't felt this bad in a long time. My fingers ran through my hair to relieve the tension on my skull, and that's when I noticed Volt was shirtless.

And he was ripped.

Every line of muscle was emphasized like it was outlined with permanent marker. His skin was flawless and tight, his strength and power obvious every time he moved. I knew he had a nice body, but I didn't realize it was *that* nice.

Volt watched me, his thoughts a mystery behind his eyes.

"Have you always been this ripped?" I blurted.

An arrogant smile stretched his lips. "Yeah."

"Oh…" I forced myself to look away because now I was just gawking.

Volt grabbed an extra pillow and stuffed it behind my back. "Get comfortable. I'll bring breakfast."

"In bed?" I asked in surprise.

"Yep." He left the bedroom for a few moments before he returned with a bed tray. He placed it over my legs. There was one plate with scrambled eggs, bacon, and two pieces of toast. In a shot glass was a little bit of water and two pink roses. After he set the tray down, he grabbed the orange juice and put it on the nightstand.

My mouth was hanging open because I was in shock. "Whoa…"

"It tastes as good as it looks."

"I just… I'm surprised."

"Hotel De La Volt is pretty classy. You should stay here more often."

"I will if I get breakfast in bed every day."

He blurted out the following word at the speed of light. "Done."

I picked up my fork and began to eat, eyeing the roses at the same time. "Where did you find these?"

"Outside. There's a rose bush." He left the bed and walked around back to his side. He got under the covers and picked up a paperback he was reading. He threw on a pair of black glasses and started reading.

I took a drink of my juice and studied him. "You wear glasses?"

He kept the book open and turned to me. "Just when I read. Sometimes, I have a hard time with the small font."

I never knew that. Surprisingly, he looked good in glasses. Somehow, he looked better. It brought out the color of his eyes and gave him a wise appearance. With his ripped body and thin hips, the glasses made him sexier than he already was. "You should wear those more often."

"Why?" This time he kept reading.

"You look cute."

"Cute?" he asked with a smile.

"I mean, they look sexy on you."

"Oh yeah?" Now his mouth was upturned in a full smile. He shut the book and turned to me. "You're into that?"

"I wouldn't say that. But they look good on you. I'm just giving you a compliment."

"Well, I appreciate that compliment. You've told me I'm hot twice in five minutes. I must be having a good hair day."

I rolled my eyes. "You always have a good hair day."

"I'm starting to think you have a thing for me." He opened the book again and turned back to the page.

"Yeah right." *Like that would ever happen.*

"Well, I think you're pretty sexy. And cute. And funny. Beautiful. Smart and fun. Woman of my dreams." He said it in a serious tone but his eyes continued to scan the words on the page.

I couldn't tell if he was being serious or not. He couldn't be because Volt didn't have those kinds of feelings for anyone. But it was such a strange thing for him to say. "I can't tell if you're joking or not." I took a bite of my toast.

"That's because I'm not."

I chewed my food and had a difficult time swallowing it because my throat was so dry. "Well, if this is a joke, I don't get it."

Volt turned the page. "Do you like your breakfast?"

"It's delicious. Thank you."

"I would have made you coffee, but it wouldn't mix well with the alcohol."

"And I already took some painkillers. Don't want to die today."

"I wouldn't want that either."

I eyed the side of the book he was reading but couldn't make out the title. "What book is that?"

"*The Count of Monte Cristo.*"

"Any good?"

"Definitely one of my favorites."

"Do you read often?"

"Every night before I go to bed."

I had no idea. "I don't read as much as I would like. I just don't have time."

"You always have time. It's just a matter of making time."

I guess I'd rather watch TV before bed than read. I kept eating my breakfast until I wiped the plate clean. The roses were fresh and lively. I didn't want to put them aside because they were so beautiful, invigorated with life even though they'd already been picked. I set the glass on the nightstand before I set the tray on the floor. "Would you judge me if I stayed and went back to sleep?"

"Nope."

"I'm not cramping your style? You don't have plans?"

He looked up, complete seriousness on his face. "You're welcome to stay as long as you like. There's nothing else I'd rather be doing right now." He turned back to his book and flipped the page.

Something felt different in the air, but I couldn't put my finger on what it was. Since I was too exhausted and sick to put too much thought into it, I lay down and closed my eyes. That's when I realized I was only wearing his shirt and my panties underneath. I couldn't recall putting on the shirt or where I got it. "Did you dress me last night?"

"No. You took off your dress, so I handed you a shirt."

"I just took off my dress?" I asked incredulously. How drunk was I?

"Don't worry, I didn't see anything. And I wouldn't have looked anyway."

"Oh really?" That wasn't the Volt I knew at all.

"I would have looked if it were someone else. Not you."

***

We played checkers in bed, and I won twice in a row.

"I'm awesome at this." I was always competitive when it came to games. It was just my nature.

25

"Yep." Volt seemed bored with the game, making lazy moves and not paying attention.

"Are you just a sore loser?"

"Did it occur to you that I'm letting you win?"

All the pride left my body. "You wouldn't..."

"Or would I?" A slight smirk was on his lips.

"But you have no reason to let me win."

"You aren't feeling well," he answered. "I do have a reason."

I narrowed my eyes in suspicion. "I don't want you to let me win."

"Alright then." He made his next move and took three of my pieces. And he reached the very end. "King me."

A growl escaped my lips.

"Now look who's a poor sport."

We spent the day playing games, napping, and eating. I hung out with Volt a lot, but I never had a day quite like this. It was nice and relaxing, and I didn't mind being in his t-shirt and sweatpants all day. He didn't take a shower or get dressed either. And he wore his glasses all day, even when he wasn't reading. I wondered if that was because of the compliment I gave him.

Volt sat beside me on the couch while we watched TV. He was still shirtless, as he'd been all day. It'd become distracting, to say the least. Sometimes, I wanted to run my fingers down his chest just to feel how hard he was. "This is the best Sunday I've had in a while."

"Yeah. It got even better when my migraine went away."

He chuckled and ran his fingers through my hair. "Maybe you'll take it easy next time."

"I didn't drink that much."

"Well, the bartender must have thought you were cute because those drinks were strong."

"The bartender was a woman."

He smiled. "Even better."

I rolled my eyes and looked at the TV. When I saw the last football game of the day come on, I realized something. "Oh shit. Today is Sunday."

His fingers paused when they were in my hair. "Yeah..."

"I'm supposed to see Sage." How could I have forgotten? "Damn, where's my clutch?"

He dropped his hand, and his eyes fell along with the movement. "On the kitchen counter."

I hopped off the couch and headed straight for it. After I pulled out my phone, I realized the screen was black.

The battery was dead.

No wonder why I hadn't heard it ring.

I grabbed Volt's phone charger and plugged it in so I could turn it on. The moment the screen came on, I got text messages from Sage.

Are we still on for tonight?

A few hours later, he texted again. *Did you get my last message?*

Then he texted me again. *Everything all right?*

I felt like such a jerk for making him worry. I was lying around Volt's house all day doing absolutely nothing. *I'm so sorry for the late reply. My phone died and I didn't even realize it.*

The three dots formed on the screen instantly, like he was waiting by the phone. *I'm just relieved you're okay. A little worried there.*

I'm sorry for stressing you out.

It's okay. As long as I get to see you tonight I'll forgive you.

I smiled. *I'm getting the check so don't bother.*

Then I'm getting a kiss.

I smiled again. *That works for me.*

I set my phone down and walked back to the couch. "I got a hold of Sage. Everything is okay."

Volt stared at the TV and didn't turn around.

"Volt?"

"That's great," he said quietly.

I thought I detected a hint of hostility in the air, but that couldn't be possible. "I'm going to head out. I need to shower and get ready for my night."

"Alright."

I changed back into my dress and heels and grabbed my clutch. I headed to the door where Volt was already standing. "Thanks for letting me crash here."
"No problem. You're welcome to stay here whenever you want." That happiness that was in his eyes just a moment before was gone. Now he seemed hollow, like he'd never find joy as long as he lived.

"Is something wrong?" One moment we were watching TV together, laughing and talking about the game. Then the next moment, he was quiet and distant.

"No." He opened the door and gestured for me to walk out. "Have a great time on your date."

I walked out. "Okay..."

"See you later." He shut the door and immediately locked it when it was closed.

It was the strangest goodbye, but if Volt really had a problem, he would come out and tell me. Perhaps he was just tired or had a hangover like I did. Maybe I was reading into things that weren't there.

So I left.

***

We sat across from each other at the table in the restaurant, and while we ate our entrees, we discussed work and music. I told Sage about my classroom and how the school year was getting easier every month—thanks to Volt.

He stared at me most of the time, but since he was so charming and handsome, it didn't feel intrusive. It seemed like I was the only woman in the room. "So, what happened today? With your phone?"

"Oh, that." The night before was a drunken blur. "It died at some point last night or this morning, but I was so hung over, I didn't even think about it."

He chuckled. "Sounds like a good night."

"Yeah. But I don't think I'll be drinking like that for a while."

"Did you sleep all day?"

"For the most part. I woke up when Volt made breakfast then I went back to sleep for a while. Then we started watching the game, and I lost track of time." His bed was unnaturally comfortable. It was like sleeping on a pile of sheep. His mattress was soft and his sheets were made of satin. I wasn't sure how he got up every morning. If it were me, I'd just lay there forever.

Sage was about to spear a piece of chicken when he stopped. "Volt made you breakfast?"

"Yeah, I didn't know he could cook either." I chuckled and kept eating.

"So, that means he was at your place?" He held his fork but didn't take another bite of his food. He stared at me quietly, his thoughts a mystery behind those hazelnut eyes.

"No. We were at his place."

"Meaning...you spent the night?" He kept his tone the same, but his eyes were full of accusation.

Now I understood what he was thinking. "No, not like that."

He released the breath he was holding.

"Well, I did sleep over. But that was because we were drinking last night, and I had way too much. So he

31

carried me to his apartment and let me crash in his bed. The next morning, he helped me get rid of my hangover. That's all." Since Volt was my best friend, I didn't think any of that was weird. Sometimes I forgot how our relationship seemed to other people who didn't know us.

"Oh... Do you do that often?"

The only other time that I had was when I tried to sleep with him. "No."

"Okay." He finally returned to eating, but he still seemed uneasy. The date wasn't as carefree as it was a moment earlier. Tension filled the air.

Maybe I shouldn't have said all of that.

But that would be lying.

Hopefully, he wouldn't ask if we slept in the same bed. Because I couldn't lie, and it would make me look like a downright ho. "Volt and I have been good friends for a while. We do a lot of stuff together."

He took a long drink of his wine. "Have you guys dated before?"

"No."

"Not once?" he asked.

"Nope. Volt isn't my type, and I'm not his either."

He stopped eating again. "Really?"

"Really what?"

"You think you aren't his type?"

"I know I'm not." He wanted a supermodel with ridiculous measurements. They had to wear skin-tight clothes at all times, and their hair had to look like they just walked out of a salon every second of the day. And he wanted something hollow and meaningless.

I didn't care about any of that stuff. Of course, I wanted good sex...but I wanted it to be good because there was so much love between my partner and I...not because he practiced on different women every night.

Sage gave me a look I've never seen before.

"What?"

"I can't tell if you're joking or not."

Why would I be joking? "Sorry?"

"It's just..." He turned back to his plate. "Never mind."

"What?" I pressed.

"Forget I said anything." He turned to the waiter and made a hand gesture to request the tab.

I wasn't even finished with my dinner.

Did I screw this up?

What did I say?

Was this over?

***

Sage walked me to my door, his hands in his pockets. "Well, thanks for having dinner with me." He kept a foot of space between us, like we were coworkers or siblings. "I'll see you around."

He was blowing me off. "Sage, hold on."

He turned back around, disappointment written on his face.

"I don't know what I said to push you away, but I'm sorry for that. Talk to me. I don't want this to end."

He rubbed his hand up the back of his neck, his fingers brushing through his hair.

"We were great at the start of dinner, but then it crashed at the end. Did I do something?"

"I just...don't want to get involved with someone who's already involved with someone else."

What was he talking about? "I don't understand your meaning."

"I know we aren't exclusive or anything, so I really have no right to feel this way. But...whatever you have with Volt seems pretty serious. Maybe if you were casually dating someone else, it wouldn't bother me. But, the fact you're sleeping over there and spending all day with him without even realizing your phone is off...makes me uneasy."

Why did I tell him about Volt at all? It was biting me in the ass. "Sage, I understand where you're coming from. But there's nothing going on between Volt and I. He really is just a friend."

"That's in love with you."

I took an involuntary breath when I heard what he said. My lips parted with a gasp and my eyes expanded to twice their normal size. His words were so ridiculous I couldn't even process them. "Sage, that's absurd."

"Is it?" he pressed.

I laughed because it was ridiculous. "Trust me, Volt doesn't see me as anything besides his annoying friend. He makes fun of me every single day, and he sleeps around with anything that moves. When we first met, he told me I was a weirdo. I think I gave you the wrong impression because of what happened last night. But I promise you, we've never done anything like that before."

"That isn't the only reason why I feel this way."

I didn't have a clue what that other reason was. "Okay..."

35

"I see the way he looks at you."

I rolled my eyes. "Volt is just protective of me. After my last boyfriend, he doesn't want me to get hurt again."

"What happened with your last boyfriend?"

I didn't want to get into it when we were just starting to date. Talk about a mood killer. "He cheated on me."

"I see..." Sage's eyes filled with sadness.

"Volt was upset about it and took matters into his own hands..." Even though Drew deserved it, I wish Volt hadn't done what he did. "And he's just worried about me getting hurt again. That's all."

Sage's shoulders started to relax and the coldness disappeared from his eyes. "I guess I can understand that."

"I'm sorry I gave you the wrong impression. But there's really nothing between Volt and I. I love him and he loves me—but in very platonic ways."

"Okay," he said. "I believe you."

I saved this date from total destruction. I just wish I wasn't stupid enough to say anything about Volt to begin with. "So...are you free on Tuesday? I'd like to take you out...so we can have a redo."

Finally, he smiled. It was the kind of joy that reached his eyes instead of staying on his lips. "I'd like that."

Crisis averted. "Great. Me too."

Chapter Three

Volt

Clay began the critical thinking part of the exam. He had to read an article and determine the tone and intention the author was trying to portray. Thankfully, we worked on the vocabulary section for a long time. Otherwise, he wouldn't have been able to read a single sentence.

My mind was somewhere else the entire time he worked. I kept thinking about the way Taylor stabbed me in the heart when she left my apartment the other day. We spent the entire Sunday lying in bed together or watching TV on the couch. She even forgot about her date until the day was nearly over.

And then she left.

Was I stupid for thinking that Sunday afternoon actually meant something? I made her breakfast in bed like I would every day if she was the woman I woke up next to. I ran my fingers through her hair and even told her how I felt about her.

But she didn't take me seriously.

Honestly, I was hoping she would forget about Sage.

And when I thought I got what I wanted, I was thrilled. Then it was taken away from me in the blink of an eye.

She didn't want to stay with me.

She wanted to go.

"Volt?"

"Hmm?" I turned back to Clay, unsure how long I'd been drifting.

"I've been trying to get your attention for, like, a minute now."

"Well, now you have it. What's up?" I ran my fingers over my temple, feeling a migraine that emerged from my heart rather than my brain.

Clay studied me, his hand still holding the corner of the page like he was going to flip it. He marked up the page with the blue pen I'd given him, underlining the parts he was unsure about as well as the key points he needed to answer the questions.

When he didn't say anything, I spoke again. "What's your question?" Over the course of the past few months, he'd dropped his smartass attitude and became more open with me. Instead of watching every move I made because he didn't trust me, he finally took down his walls and

40

breathed easily around me. He was a different kid altogether.

"Seems like something is bothering you. Did I do something?" The vulnerability in his voice, something he never let escape, crushed me.

"No. Not at all, Clay." This kid had become an essential part of my existence. When I wasn't with him, I worried about him, particularly on the weekends. I wondered if his father was treating him well. I always gave him money on Friday so he could get through the weekend, and I just hoped it was enough. I cared about him more than I could stand. It was the kind of concern that actually hurt. "There's something else on my mind..."

"You want to talk about it?"

"No, it's okay." I wasn't talking about my love life with a sixteen-year-old.

"Oh... I thought we were friends."

"We are friends," I said quickly.

"Well, I tell you stuff...but you don't tell me stuff." He looked down at the page and picked up his pen again.

He was right. This was a two-way street. And I suspected he didn't have any friends besides me. "It's about a girl."

He looked up again, interested.

"I...kinda have a thing for her, but she doesn't notice me."

"Been there, done that."

"I'm not sure what to do about it."

"How can she not notice you?" he asked with a laugh. "You're good-looking and rich. What else can a girl want?"

I smiled. "Did you just give me a compliment?"

"Uh...shit. I did."

"Hey. What did I say about cussing?"

He rolled his eyes.

"And looks and wealth don't matter when it comes to women."

"That's a load of crap."

"Well, they don't matter when it comes to *this* woman." Taylor cared more about inner beauty than anything else, and I seriously lacked in that department. She'd only seen the ugly side of me, the broken man that had his heart ripped out of his chest. I turned ice-cold after I got my heart shattered, and that's all she'd ever known. If we met before all of that happened, things would have been different. Much different.

"What does this woman want?"

"A nice guy." In a nutshell.

"But you are a nice guy."

"Not really." I was selfish and superficial. I was the first one to admit all my faults. Taylor was out of my league, and I knew it.

"I think so," Clay said. "No one has ever paid any attention to me...at least in a good way. You help me every day after school and give me food. No one cares about me except you."

His words were both beautiful and devastating. "Clay, that's not true."

"Yes, it is," he whispered. "And we both know it." He turned back to the page and kept his eyes averted.

"Your teachers care about you—"

"They hate me. I'm just some annoying poor kid that sits in the back of the class."

"And your father—"

"He only uses me to get money from the government. And he pisses it away on drugs and liquor. He doesn't care whether I live or die."

How this kid was still going floored me. He was in my office, trying to make a better life for himself. After saying all of that, I'm not sure where he got the motivation. "I'm sure you have friends who care about you."

He shook his head. "I'm on my own."

There I was complaining that I couldn't be with the one woman I actually wanted while Clay was fighting to survive every single day. I didn't know true misery, not like him. "You're never on your own, Clay. You always have me."

***

Clay grabbed his rusty bike from the bike rack, and we walked up the sidewalk together.

"How about we get you a new bike?" It didn't look like it would last much longer. It was rusty and old, and the chain popped off every two seconds.

"No, it's okay."

"I really don't mind, Clay."

"If I come home with a new bike, Dad will wonder where I got it. It's just best to leave it alone."

His dad wouldn't want his son to have something nice? I would never understand those kind of parents. I've heard of them before, but I've never been in so deep like I was now. "Let me know if you change your mind."

"It's easier having crappy stuff anyway. I never have to worry about someone stealing it. When you don't have nice things, people leave you alone."

An Aston Martin was sitting in my garage at that very moment. It was a beautiful car I hardly ever drove, but I had the wealth to afford something I didn't even need.

Now I hated that car.

And I hated myself for owning it.

"Want to get something to eat?" I didn't have time to pick up food before our study meeting.

He shrugged. He never asked for anything even though I made it clear I'd get him anything he wanted.

"How about Mega Shake?" It was just at the end of the block.

"Cool," he said. "I love that place." There was a skip in his step when he knew he was getting dinner.

And that made me sad.

"Volt?"

I could recognize that voice anywhere. It was in my dreams, and when I was awake, it echoed in my mind.

I turned around and saw Taylor standing there. She had her big bag over her shoulder, and she wore a light blue dress with a pink cardigan. Her clothes were always two sizes too big and didn't highlight all of her natural curves. Sometimes I wondered if she was specifically trying to hide them.

Her hair fell over one shoulder, like always. A breathtaking smile was on her lips, making her eyes crinkle in the corners. Standing right in front of me was the one woman I wanted but couldn't have. I hadn't gotten laid in so long I couldn't remember the last time it happened. I had every right to go out and snag a beautiful woman, but there was no one else I wanted.

I only wanted her.

She came up to me with that smile still on her lips.

I forgot where I was and what I was doing, just standing there in awe. When I looked at her, I froze on the spot, unable to determine reality from fiction. She made me nervous and awkward at the same time.

She turned me into a different man entirely.

"You all right?" she asked when she was just a foot away.

I snapped out of my daydream and cleared my throat. "Sorry, the sun was at a weird angle...couldn't really see." The sun was setting the opposite way, but I needed something to say.

She didn't challenge me. "What are you up to?"

"Uh..." I couldn't remember, actually.

Clay chuckled from beside me.

And that's when I fell back into place. "Clay and I were about to get something to eat."

Clay laughed again, knowing I was acting like a total idiot. "Yeah. We're going to Mega Shake. Wanna come?"

He hated any adult he met, so I knew he understood exactly who Taylor was.

Taylor looked at him, and whatever affection she had for me was amplified tenfold for him. "I've heard so much about you, Clay. It's great to meet you." She extended her hand and shook his.

"You've heard that I'm a super smart and good-looking stud?" he asked with a grin.

Taylor laughed. "Yes. That's exactly what I heard."

"I teach Volt the ways of my charm—whenever I have time." He was still sitting on his bike with his backpack hanging off his shoulders.

"That's very nice of you." Taylor was immediately smitten with him, just like she was with all of her students.

It was nice having Clay there because the focus was taken off of me.

"Let's get something to eat." Clay turned his bike and started pushing it toward the restaurant. "I'm starving."

"Good call." Taylor trailed behind him and walked beside me.

I put my hands in my pockets, feeling out of place standing so close to her. I could smell the usual scent of vanilla and oranges from her soft hair. I could feel the bristle of the breeze every time she moved. I was innately aware of every little thing she did, even when she took an innocent breath.

I couldn't believe there was ever a time when I didn't feel like this.

We walked into the diner and ordered our food before we sat down in the booth. Taylor sat beside me, and Clay sat across from us. He kept looking at Taylor, just as interested in her as I was.

"What do you do for money?" Clay asked as he ate his fries.

"What do I do for money?" Taylor asked with confusion.

"Yeah," Clay said. "What's your job?"

"I'm a teacher," Taylor said. "I teach at Bristol Academy."

Clay grimaced. "Bunch of preppies…"

"Clay," I warned him. "Don't be rude."

"I'm not being rude," Clay said. "Kids who go to private school are preppies. Everyone knows that."

Instead of being annoyed, Taylor continued the conversation. "Those kids in private school aren't any different than you."

"Whatever," Clay said. "They're a bunch of smart, rich kids."

"You're smart too."

"Am not," Clay argued.

"That's not what Volt tells me." She smiled as she looked at Clay.

The conversation started to feel comfortable, and without thinking twice about it, I rested my arm over the back of her chair, touching Taylor on the nape of her neck.

I realized my mistake, but it was too late to fix it. At least she didn't notice anything.

"Really?" Clay asked, his eyes moving to mine.

"What can I say?" I said with a shrug. "I talk about you."

"And say bad things?" Clay pressed.

"Nothing but good things," Taylor said. "He's very fond of you." She smeared her fries in ketchup then popped them into her mouth.

I'd give anything to be those fries.

Clay asked her more questions about the school she taught at, and then the conversation turned to the SAT. They got along well, better than Clay and I got along when we first met. Taylor had a natural aura that made people feel comfortable in her presence. Perhaps it was a maternal atmosphere. Or maybe it was the way she spoke. I didn't know.

Maybe she cast a spell on all of us.

Clay finished eating then pushed his tray away. "I better get home. Thanks for dinner, Volt."

He always said thank you. And that was something I didn't need to teach him. He was proud and stubborn, but he was grateful and appreciative. That's how I knew he was a good kid underneath all that street talk. "You're welcome, Clay."

"Nice to meet you, Lady." He winked then walked out.

When he was out of our sight, Taylor turned to me. "He's cute."

"Just don't tell him that." He wouldn't like that description one bit.

"I understand why you're so determined to help him."

"He's a good kid in a bad situation."

"I see what you mean." She finished her food then picked at a few of my fries.

If someone else ate off my plate, I'd be annoyed. But this woman could do whatever she wanted. And she definitely was doing whatever she wanted.

"Any bruises?"

"I haven't seen any in awhile."

"Good." She sighed in relief. "I'm glad he has someone watching over him."

It was sad that I was the only one. "Everyone needs someone. And I'm his someone."

"You know what?" She turned to me, those beautiful blue eyes sucking me in. "You're my someone."

"Yeah?" We were close to each other in the booth, close enough that I could kiss her if I had the balls to do it. I kissed her the other night and felt her kiss me back. Why couldn't we do that now? Why couldn't we do that all the time? Why couldn't we do that for the rest of our lives?

Shit, I was in deep.

"Yeah," she said. "You're my someone. You know, that person I can always rely on to look out for me."

"And you're my someone." *My only someone.*

"Good thing we have each other." She turned back to my tray and ate a few more fries.

Why could we have these conversations but not be something more? How could she sit this close to me in a booth but not feel what I feel? How did those feelings just disappear? How could she date someone else?

I wanted to ask about Sage, but I didn't want to hear her answer. What I really wanted was for her to say they weren't seeing each other anymore. That would be the best news I've heard in a while. "How was your date?"

"It was okay."

Okay? That didn't sound good. Was I an asshole for being excited by that answer? "Something go wrong?"

"We just got into an argument over something stupid..."

"Such as?"

She shook it off. "Nothing important. But we're going out again on Tuesday."

Ugh. What a tease. "Did you sleep with him?"

What the hell was wrong with me?

Why did I ask these questions when I didn't want the answers?

Why was I torturing myself?

"No," she answered. "On our last date, he wanted to come inside, but I didn't want to rush it. We've only seen each other a few times. I went too fast with Drew and looked what happened there."

I seized the opportunity. "You're right. You should go slow. Like, really slow. Maybe even wait until marriage."

She laughed because she thought I was joking. "Maybe even wear a chastity belt."

"Even better. Wear it at all times, just in case."

She laughed harder. "I'll just hide it under my clothes and wear it when I'm in my bikini. People won't think that's weird."

"I think it's the best idea I've ever heard." As long as she gave me the key to unlock it.

Her chuckles died down. "What have you been up to?"

"Nothing much." *Just hating life.*

"No ladies?"

"Nope."

"That has to be a record for you. What's it been? A few weeks?"

"A month, actually." I'd been jerking off a lot—thinking of that night she and I fooled around.

"Is everything okay?" She crossed her legs then faced me again.

"Yeah...just haven't been in the mood lately."

"Do you go through these phases often?"

Never. "Every once in a while."

"Well, at least you'll really enjoy the sex when you put yourself out there again."

The idea of having sex with anyone but her didn't seem appealing at all. It would be another meaningless night with a random woman. With Taylor, kissing her was more exciting than any hot sex I've ever had. It was full of passion and desire. And it was sexy as hell.

That's what I wanted. "How's your classroom doing?"

"Good," she said. "I'm giving them another exam soon. This time, I'm doing it my way."

"Be careful with that."

"That last exam was way too easy. They need something more complicated."

"What about a field trip?" I was just relieved we weren't talking about my sex life anymore. Because when I thought about sex, I thought about her. And that made me hard in my jeans, and it would be impossible to cover up—if she looked.

"I haven't done one yet."

"It's almost the end of the first semester, and you haven't done a field trip yet?" That was bound to piss off some parents.

"There just hasn't been time."

"You need to make time." *Like, ASAP.*

"I don't know...then I have to get chaperones."

"I'll be a chaperone. You only have twelve students, so two adults should be fine."

"Really?" she asked. "They won't think it's weird a random guy is volunteering for a school field trip?"

I wasn't just a guy. "It won't be a problem. Remember, I used to be a teacher."

"Oh yeah." She smacked herself in the forehead. "Sometimes I forget."

"Let's schedule one. How about the Planetarium?"

"Ooh...that could be cool."

We could sit together in the dark. I could innocently touch her hand and imagine she was touching mine in the same way. If we had enough quality time together underneath the projected stars, maybe she would look at me differently.

Maybe she would forget about Sage.

***

"Hey, dear. How are you?" Mom spoke into my ear over the phone.

I was sitting at my desk at work. "Good. How are you?"

"Great. My shop is closing down since the holidays are just around the corner. I keep asking your father to take me to Paris, but he won't budge..."

"He'll come around, Mom." I put my feet on the desk and closed my eyes, wanting this conversation to end. I suspected my love life would come up—because it always came up.

"Will you be driving up with us this weekend?"

"This weekend?" *Driving up with them where?*

"To Suzie's wedding. You don't remember?"

It totally slipped my mind. I didn't care much for weddings. I couldn't be myself at family weddings because that was just weird. "Now I do."

"Well, Paul's daughter is going to be there. She's actually sitting at our table."

Oh no. My parents were setting me up on another blind date. They were the worst. Most of them were super conservative debutantes, and that definitely wasn't my type.

"Volt?"

I could get out of this forced date by not going to the wedding at all. But that would make me look like a huge dick when I already said I was coming. The only other alternative was to bring someone.

Taylor.

The light bulb went on in my head, and I just went with it. "I'm bringing someone." Taylor would come along if I asked her to. She loved food, people, and dancing. A wedding would be perfect for her. And there's no one else I'd rather go with.

Mom was dead silent before the gasp came. "You're bringing someone?" Her voice was louder by tenfold and her excitement bubbled like a newly opened bottle of champagne. "Volt, that's absolutely wonderful. I'm so excited to meet her. I'm sure she's amazing."

She is amazing.

"Tell me about her."

"Her name is Taylor."

"Awe...beautiful. How long have you been dating?"

"We're just friends, Mom."

"Oh, okay." She was rolling her eyes through the phone. I could actually hear it. "Your father and I won't scare her off."

Better not. "I'll see you on Saturday then."

"Alright. I'm looking forward to seeing you, baby."

My mom still called me baby. But what was I supposed to do? Ask her to stop? She's my mom. I can't do that. "I can't wait to see you too."

"Love you, baby."

There she goes again. "Love you too."

***

Clay didn't open his notebook like he usually did. He fell into the chair across from me and gave me a mischievous grin. He had a trick up his sleeve, and I suspected I wouldn't like it.

"What?" I asked.

"Volt and Taylor sitting in a tree...k-i-s-s-i-n-g—"

"Are you five?"

"You act like such a loser around her."

If Clay noticed it, then she must have too. And that was the most mortifying thing ever. I had the smoothest moves when it came to women, but all of those plays went out the window when Taylor stole my heart. Now I could barely say hello to her. "I admit I'm a little off my game."

"Off your game?" Clay laughed. "You look like a stupid buffoon when you stare at her like that."

"I know." He didn't need to tell me twice.

"How does she not notice?"

"I don't—" That last sentence gave me some hope. "You don't think she notices?"

"Nah. She's totally blind."

Was I really taking comfort in the observations of a sixteen-year-old? "That's a relief."

"Why don't you just ask her out?"

"Because..."

"Because why?" he pressed.

"She doesn't see me like that. I'm just a friend to her."

"And isn't asking her out on a date a good way to show her otherwise?"

"But she'll say no, and it'll be weird."

Clay stared at me like he didn't understand me at all. "I don't get it. I thought real men weren't scared of anything?"

"They aren't, but…it's complicated."

"Complicated how?"

"Because she's my friend. And if I make a stupid move, she might stop being my friend."

"I don't have many friends," he said. "But I always assumed they were your friend no matter what?"

"Well…yeah."

"Then go for it. She's cute."

"I know she is." I noticed it every damn day. "But she's seeing someone."

"Oh…she has a boyfriend?"

"Not a boyfriend. They aren't serious—at least not yet."

"Then you can do something."

Clay was too young to understand. "If I did, that would make me an asshole."

"Hey, watch the language."

I chuckled when I realized I shoved my own foot in my mouth. "You got me."

"Why would that make you an asshole? And yes, I can cuss that one time because you just cussed."

He had a good argument, so I let it slide. "It sounds like she really likes him. And if that's how she feels, it would be disrespectful to step in and ruin something that could turn into something that she wants."

Clay stared at me blankly.

"I couldn't do that to her."

"You love her, right?"

Love was a strong word, and I wasn't ready to say it. I wasn't sure how I felt. "I don't want to be with anyone but her. I haven't felt this way since... Well, it's been a while."

"Since what?" he asked.

I wasn't sure why I was telling Clay any of this. He was my student, but he was also...something more. I wouldn't consider him to be a friend. I guess he was...like a son. "I was with this girl for a while, and I was going to ask her to marry me. But I found out she was sleeping around."

"That sucks."

"Yeah, it did." *It was brutal.*

"And you've been single ever since?"

61

"Yeah. It's hard for me to trust people."

"And you trust her?"

I trusted her more than anyone else on the planet. "She would never hurt me."

"Then you have to do something—whether she's seeing someone or not."

"But she doesn't feel the same way. I would just make her uncomfortable, mess up our friendship, and ruin her relationship with this guy."

"But if you told her how you felt, maybe she would feel something for you."

Or maybe not. "I'm going to wait it out and see how it goes. If she breaks up with this guy, I'll make a move."

"You better. Stop acting like a pussy."

"Whoa, watch your mouth."

Clay didn't regret what he said. "Sometimes, you need someone to light a fire under your—"

"Don't say it."

"Tushy." He rolled his eyes. "And you clearly need a fire under yours."

***

I texted Taylor as I walked home. *Baby, you busy?* I growled to myself when I realized what I wrote and how fluidly I dropped the nickname. I erased the word before I sent the message. *You busy?*

Just got home. What's up?

Can I come by? I was already outside her apartment.

Sure. I'll throw a bag of popcorn in the microwave.

Excellent thinking, baby. Ugh, I did it again. *Excellent thinking.*

See you in a few.

I took the elevator to her floor then knocked. My heart was racing in my chest, and I tried to keep my breathing regulated. She did strange things to me. Made me *feel* strange things.

She opened the door still wearing her school clothes. She wore a long dress that had zebras on it with leggings underneath. A black scarf was around her neck to keep the incoming fall chill away. "Hey. The popcorn is done."

"Then I got here right on time." I walked inside and stopped myself from hugging her. "How was your day?"

"Good." She opened the bag of popcorn then plopped down onto the couch. "Clay is a really great kid."

"He is, huh?" I sat beside her and shoved my hand inside the bag.

She threw a few pieces into the air and caught them in her mouth. "You can tell he's a smart guy. He just hasn't been educated well."

"You hit the nail right on the head." Clay was wiser than most kids. He understood how the world really worked, and he knew how to survive. Most kids didn't understand that kind of pressure. Their motivation stemmed from desire, not hunger.

"He's so fond of you. I can tell."

"Yeah..." We did have a good relationship. I could tell he looked up to me in a lot of ways. And I could tell he trusted me.

"He's lucky to have you." She wrapped her arm through mine and gave me a squeeze.

Even that got me hot.

I loved it when she touched me.

I wanted her to keep touching me.

"Thanks."

She turned back to the bag of popcorn, crunching every piece in that tiny mouth of hers.

"Hey, I was wondering if you could do me a favor."

"Sure. Anything you want, I'm there." She turned her full attention on me, still shoving popcorn into her mouth.

She made eating popcorn sexy as hell. "I have this wedding to go to this Saturday, and I want you to come as my date."

"A wedding?"

"It's my cousin's wedding."

"Oh…" Instead of agreeing right away, she remained apprehensive.

"I talked to my mom today, and she has plans to set me up with some family friend…so I told her I was already bringing someone." Hopefully, that wasn't too forward. Blind dates arranged by my parents were the worst.

"She's trying to set you up with someone?" she asked in surprise.

"My mom is pretty adamant about me taking a wife."

She chuckled. "Wow. That's brutal."

"So, you'll come with me?" *Please come with me.*

"Uh…" She turned away, her mind distracted by something else.

"You don't have to if you don't want to. Honestly, there's no pressure. I could just bring someone else. It's not a big deal."

"Who would you bring?"

I didn't want to bring anyone else. In that case, I'd rather go alone. "I don't know…one of my regulars."

"But won't they think things are getting serious? You know, since they're meeting your family?"

"Uh…I hope not."

"No, I'll go."

Thank god. "Are you sure?"

"Yeah."

"You don't have plans already?" *With that stupid asshole.*

"No. I'd love to go with you." She settled back in the couch beside me. "Now I have to go shopping."

"For what?"

"Something to wear."

"You already have plenty of stuff."

"But I don't have many nice dresses—the kind you wear to a wedding."

"What's wrong with what you wear every day?"

"You're the first person who made fun of me for it."

Now, I didn't understand why I ever teased her. She looked beautiful in everything. She had the kind of beauty that thudded constantly. It didn't matter what she wore or how she did her hair and makeup, she just looked perfect. "I was a jerk. Taylor, you rock everything you wear. Honestly."

She smiled. "Aww. You just gave me a compliment."

I would give her compliments for the rest of her life—if she would be mine. "And I meant it."

Chapter Four

Taylor

I was dreading this.

Like, super duper.

I made the call and listened to the phone ring. "Don't pick up. Don't pick up."

But of course, he did. "Hey." Sage's voice came across the phone. "What's going on?"

"Nothing much. How about you?" I started pacing in my apartment, feeling my heart pound with adrenaline.

"Just got home from the gym. Hearing your voice is a nice reward for working out so hard."

I was too nervous to crack a smile. "I would have loved to see that."

He chuckled, his voice deep and hypnotizing. "Have plans tonight?"

"No. I'm free. I was hoping we could do something."

"Yeah, sure. Two nights in a row, I'm down with that."

Here it goes. "Well, I actually need to cancel tomorrow..." I knew this was going to blow up into a fight. I could sense it. Sage and I weren't even official yet, and the relationship was tense.

"Oh. Everything alright?"

"Yeah. I told Volt I would go to a wedding with him, like, six weeks ago, and I totally forgot." A little white lie didn't hurt anyone, right? "His mom keeps trying to set him up, and he thinks she'll back off if he has a date."

Silence.

He was pissed. I knew it.

Sage sighed into the phone. "Well, if you committed, you committed, right?"

Really? He wasn't mad? "Yeah. I can't leave him hanging."

"I'm free tonight, so no harm done. Want to get some dinner?"

"Absolutely." That went over much smoother than I anticipated.

"Just let me hop in the shower."

"Ooh...can I watch?"

He chuckled. "I'd love that."

***

"Where is this wedding?" Sage drank his beer as he sat across from me.

"Uh...not sure. Connecticut, I think?"

"You don't know?" he asked playfully.

"All I heard was free food and open bar." Actually, I didn't hear any of those things, but I hoped it was true. My fingers were wrapped tightly around the stem of my glass.

"That's necessary at any wedding...if they want people to go."

"Well, I like weddings anyway. They're fun and happy."

"So, Volt can't get his own date?"

I suspected his irritation would flare up eventually. "No, he can." That was never the problem. "He doesn't want to take one of his regulars to a wedding because they'll think things are getting serious. He has to avoid that."

"One of his regulars?"

"Yeah. He's a terminal bachelor." I chose not to believe that. When he met the right woman, he would be saddled and subdued. But until then, he was a wild bronco.

"A player?"

"That's another word for it. He likes playing the field and doing what he wants. He refuses to have a relationship."

"Why is that?"

He never told me. "I'm not sure, but I think he got his heart broken sometime in the past."

71

"He's never told you?"

I shook my head.

"I thought you were best friends."

"We are. But he doesn't talk about that sort of stuff with me. I don't think he talks about that stuff with anyone, actually."

"Sounds like whatever happened was pretty brutal."

"Yeah…" She must have left Volt for another man or cheated on him. I wasn't sure which. Maybe it was both. "Anyway, I'm his date for the evening."

"Is that why you've never hooked up?"

Well, we kinda had hooked up. "What do you mean?"

"Because he's a player. You don't seem like the type of girl who's into that."

"I guess. But I also think we're better friends than lovers."

Sage seemed to be coming around after his outburst over Volt. Maybe he finally realized there was nothing to feel threatened by. "So you've tried to be lovers before?"

"Uh…no." I wasn't sure how to answer that. We did kiss one time, but I was delirious with pain. Volt stopped me from doing something I'd regret so it didn't count. But I changed the subject anyway just to avoid the conversation. "When was the last time you were in a relationship?"

"About a year ago." He drank his beer and kept his eyes glued to me. He had the features of a classically handsome man, someone you would see on TV. "It was a mutual parting. Just wasn't working."

"Sometimes that happens."

"Ever since then, I've been dating here and there...trying to find someone new. You'd think it'd be easy in a big city like this but it's just the opposite. There are so many choices that people can't make up their minds."

That sounded like Volt. "I know what you mean." Despite what Drew did, he did seem like a good guy. Maybe the temptation was just too much. There were too many beautiful women in the city for him to keep his hands to himself.

"There are a lot of beautiful people here," he said. "But it's very rare to find a beautiful soul." He clanked his beer against my glass. "And I think we've both found that."

***

"What are you going to tell your parents?" I walked beside Volt in my burgundy dress with sleeves and black-heeled shoes. It was a sunny day, but the chill had crept in.

73

"What do you mean?" He walked beside me with his hands in the pockets of his suit. It was charcoal gray and of the finest material. He looked taller in the clothing and somehow broader.

"Are you going to tell them I'm your girlfriend?"

"Why would I say that?"

"To get them off your back."

"I just told them we were friends…" His eyes drifted away, and they became darker like he was thinking of something only he would understand. He turned back to me, a different look on his face. "You're okay with pretending to be my girlfriend?"

"Sure. Why not?" What could be the harm in that? His parents would hear what they wanted, and Volt would be off the hook for at least a few months. "Just don't stick your tongue down my throat and we're good."

"Dang…" He gave me a teasing smile. "I wanted to play some serious tonsil hockey with you."

I rolled my eyes because I knew he was joking. "I'm sure Sage would love that."

"What he doesn't know won't hurt him."

I rolled my eyes again.

Volt grabbed my hand when we reached the front door. His fingers interlocked with mine immediately, like we held hands all the time. He pulled me in close to his side. "My parents are nice. You'll like them."

"I'm sure I will." They raised a fine son, so I was sure they were good people.

The door opened, and his mother greeted us with a smile. She had dark brown hair just like Volt, and she had his eyes too. She was a petite woman, barely five feet tall. The fact she gave birth to a six foot two man was oddly cute. "Hello, dear." His mother pulled him in for a hug. "I've missed you."

Volt hugged his mother without any embarrassment. "Missed you too, Mom."

She squeezed his hips tightly, pushing the air out of his stomach.

"Whoa, Mom. You've been hitting the weights, haven't you?"

She pulled away then patted his cheek gently. "Those wedding dresses are heavy."

Volt pulled me to his side. "Mom, this is Taylor."

She looked at me like I was a miracle sent from the heavens. Her eyes sparkled with absolute joy, and it seemed like she wanted to squeeze me just the way she did to her son. "You're so beautiful, dear." She hugged me with the same motherly affection, but thankfully, she didn't break my ribs.

Volt rolled his eyes.

"We're so glad you could come." His mother pulled away and cupped my cheeks. "Please call me Vivian."

"It's nice to meet you, Vivian. Thank you for letting me come along."

"No. Thank you." She squeezed my shoulders before she entered the house. "So...I have some bad news."

"What?" Volt asked as he stepped in with me.

"Your father is very sick," Vivian explained. "He won't be able to come."

"Sick, how?" Volt asked. "Is he okay?"

"He has food poisoning," she said. "He's been lying on the bathroom tile all day."

"Aww... I feel so bad for him." *Food poisoning was the worst.*

"Poor guy," Volt said. "Maybe we should stay home and look after him."

Vivian shook her head. "I offered, but he was insistent that we go without him. He said he's just going to be throwing up anyway. Not much we can do."

"I guess we'll only be gone for a few hours." Volt eyed his watch. "He won't be alone too long."

"That's very true." Vivian grabbed her purse from the counter. "We should get going."

***

After the ceremony was over, we took our seats at the round tables underneath the almond trees. The flowers were in full bloom, and white candles glowed from all the tables.

Volt sat beside me, and his hand immediately moved to my thigh under the table. He was adamant about keeping up appearances, even if no one could really see his hand on my leg.

I noticed a lot of women looked Volt's way, probably hoping he would be single for the evening. Some of the bridesmaids made eyes at him, and the women sitting at different tables kept casting looks his way.

Maybe bringing me was a mistake.

Vivian turned her attention on me. "Taylor, what do you do for a living?"

"I'm a teacher."

Her eyes lit up in affection. I clearly gave the right answer. "Elementary school?"

"Actually, high school," I answered. "This is my first year teaching."

"Volt used to be a teacher," Vivian said. "It's such a great profession."

"I couldn't agree more." Even though I was seriously struggling with it.

"Where do you teach?" she asked.

Volt suddenly stood up and extended his hand to me. "Dance with me."

Volt danced?

Vivian didn't seem to mind being interrupted. She was just happy her son finally had a girlfriend. "This is such a great song."

I took his palm, and he pulled me onto the dance floor. It was a slow song, one of those cheesy romance ballads that people played on their anniversary. He pulled me to his chest and rested his hands on the small of my back, keeping me tightly against him.

My arms linked around his neck. His cologne washed over me, smelling exactly like he always did. I recognized it from the scent of his sheets and his clothes. The smell was potent and made me think of that lazy Sunday we spent together. It made me think of all the times we were together, his smell infecting my memories.

Volt looked down at me with a dreamy look in his eyes. They were linked to mine, and he hardly blinked. He guided me from side to side without ever taking his eyes off me.

"You're good at that."

"At what?" he whispered.

"That sexy, dreamy look. You use that on all the girls?"

"Not really." He pulled me closer into him, his forehead touching mine.

We'd never had this kind of affection before. It was even more intimate than the heated foreplay we had a few months ago. Our lips weren't touching, and we were fully clothed, but it was still unnerving. We looked like two people madly in love, thinking about our own wedding day in the future.

I swallowed the lump in my throat to clear the tension. I felt shivers run up my spine. My hair stood on end.

Then I remembered this was all an act. Just a show.

And that made me forget about all the sensations circling through my body.

"Your mom seems happy."

"She's over the moon," he whispered. "When you aren't around, she's going to start pestering me about marriage and bullshit like that."

"That's sweet."

"I know she means well, but it annoys me sometimes."

"I understand."

"The fact she owns a wedding dress shop doesn't help. She's even more obsessed with marriage than most women."

"She owns a wedding dress shop?" I asked incredulously. "That's so cool."

He chuckled. "You're obsessed with weddings too?"

"I wouldn't say obsessed...but I think about mine."

"Yeah?" he asked. "What'll your wedding be like?"

I felt embarrassment spread through my veins. I sounded like a dumb schoolgirl that only cared about marriage and babies. "You don't want to know..."

"Would I have asked if I didn't?" He grabbed one hand and placed it over his chest as he continued to dance with me.

"You promise you won't make fun of me?"

His eyes softened. "I promise."

"Well...I've always wanted to get married outside. You know, somewhere with lots of trees, grass, and flowers. I'm more of a nature person than a church person."

"I've picked up on that."

"And I want it to be small—a hundred people or less."

"Why?"

"I just don't want it to be too big. You know, just our most intimate friends and family."

"That sounds nice. What about the guy?"

"What do you mean?"

"What'll he be like?"

"I don't know. I haven't met him yet."

He squeezed my hand gently. "How do you picture him?"

"Handsome, sweet, kind...my best friend." When our eyes locked, I felt the tension suddenly rise. My choice of words wasn't the best, but now that I said it, I couldn't take it back.

"I think that's a good description." The song came to an end but he continued to hold me. A fast-paced song came over the speakers, and people were jumping around, having a good time. But we remained idle on the dance floor, just staring at each other. "And I don't think it's funny."

"Well, thanks for not making fun of me."

"I never make fun of you."

"Oh, whatever."

"When was the last time I teased you about something?"

"Just the other day…" I drew a blank because I couldn't actually think of anything.

A victorious smile crept over his lips. "See? I told you so."

***

"This cake is so fucking good." I shoved enormous pieces into my mouth as we stood near the bar. I forgot about everyone else at that wedding and just enjoyed the arousing relationship with my piece of cake.

Volt watched me devour the whole thing. Of course, he didn't take a piece himself. "That's hot."

"Oh, shut up."

"I feel like I'm watching porn right now."

I gave him a light kick in the shin.

He came closer to me and grabbed my ass, giving it a playful squeeze. "Two can play that game."

"Whoa, what are you doing?" I took a step back.

"What?" he asked innocently. "You're my girlfriend. I'm supposed to grab your ass."

"That's not even kinda romantic."

"Real relationships aren't about being romantic all the time. They're about taking something you want without any explanation. They're about those hot quickies in the bathroom. They're about making each other come with just your fingers. Now that's a real relationship." He gave my ass a playful pat before he pulled his hand away.

Images of us screwing in the bathroom or getting each other off with just our hands flashed across my mind, and I felt heat enter my cheeks until it burned. I remembered the make out session we had in his apartment. It was something I could never forget because it ignited my body and brought it to life. I hadn't thought about it in a while, and now that I did, I felt the arousal return.

I shook it off then grabbed his ass and gave it a squeeze. "How do you like it?"

He grinned from ear to ear. "I'm always down for a little ass play."

"Oh my god," I said as I rolled my eyes.

"What?" he asked. "You've never gotten any?"

"Any what?" What was he talking about?

"Some ass play. Anal? Not ringing any bells?"

I was drawing a blank. "I like sex. You know, the regular kind."

"Then you don't know what you're missing. I'll show you sometime."

"What?" I blurted.

"Kidding." He winked at me. "Or am I?"

"I hope you're kidding. Because this is an exit only."

"They all say that...until they try it."

"I'm not letting anyone fuck—" I shut my mouth when Vivian walked over.

"You two are so cute together." Her hands were held to her chest. "I never thought my little Mur—"

"Mom, don't you dare."

Don't dare what?

"Oh, sorry," she said with a sigh. "It's a great name. I don't know why you're ashamed of it."

"What's a great name?" Volt told me his middle name but never his first name.

"Nothing," Volt said quickly. "Mom has had too much to drink, clearly."

"Have not," she said in offense.

"Mom, how about a glass of champagne?" Volt asked. "Maybe a glass of wine from the bar?"

"I'll take some champagne, please."

"Coming right up." Volt walked to the bar.

When it was just her and I, she gave me that same look again. As if I was the answer to all her prayers. If she could squeeze me again, she would. "Thank you for making my son happy. I was worried about him."

Now I felt guilty as hell. He and I were both lying to her, making her believe something that wasn't real and never would be real. One day, he would have to tell her we weren't seeing each other anymore. Would that break her heart? I really didn't feel so good about this. "Volt is a great guy."

"And you must be an amazing woman to get my son to come back around. He lost his way for a while, and I was

85

afraid he would never find himself again. But seeing the way he looks at you... I know this is it."

This is what? "Uh, Vivian..."

"He loves you. It's written all over his face every second you're by his side. He's happy, and that makes me so happy. So, thank you for being patient with him and for making my son smile again."

I didn't know what to say. Should I tell her the truth and break her heart? Could I really carry that kind of weight? Should I keep lying to her? This scheme was a bad idea. We never should have done it.

Volt returned with a glass of champagne for his mother. Then he handed me a glass as well. "They had pinot noir. I thought you would like some."

It was my favorite kind of wine. I wasn't even sure how he knew that. "Thank you." I took a long drink and tried to cover up my unease.

"Well, I'll let the two of you get back to it..." She winked at her son before she walked away.

Volt sighed when she was gone. "See what I mean? She's obsessed with—"

"I thought I could do this, but I can't."

"Do what?"

"Lie to your mother. She just came over here and told me how happy she is we're together. Volt, can you really do this to your mom? Because when you tell her we're broken up, she'll be devastated."

"Why do I have to tell her we broke up?"

"Well, eventually you will."

"Again, why? We can keep up pretenses. It's not like I see my parents all the time."

"You want to keep up a lie like this indefinitely?"

"Why does it have to be a lie? Why can't we make it real?"

Now I was lost. "What?"

"Look, this arrangement makes my parents happy. It makes me happy. There's no harm."

"Well, I'm going to get married someday, and I don't think my husband is going to be thrilled about this."

He took a long drink of his wine, unusually long. "We'll cross that bridge when we come to it, alright? For now, just leave it alone."

"When you settle down with the right girl, they're going to dislike her since they'll be attached to me. How is that fair to her?"

"I'm never going to settle down, so there's no problem there."

"Yes, you will. When you meet the right girl, you will."

"Well, I already met her, and she doesn't want me. So no, that's not going to happen." He stared at me hard, barely blinking and looking so devastated it was actually painful.

Volt was finally opening up to me, telling me his darkest secret at the most unsuspecting moment. "You've been in love before…but she didn't want you?"

He kept up his ice-cold stare before he finally turned away. "No… Forget I said anything."

"Talk to me."

"No. Just forget it." He downed the rest of his glass before setting it on a nearby table. "Let's just keep going with the plan. End of story."

"But—"

"End of story."

***

Volt was tense for the next few hours. We spent that time drinking at our table and making small talk with his family members. He didn't touch me for a while, and then his hand eventually snaked back to my thigh. I didn't push it away because I didn't want to start another fight.

Since he and I weren't talking, I spent a lot of extra time drinking the never-ending bottles of wine. My eyes began to droop, and I felt a little sluggish. I knew I had too much to drink after I already had way too much to drink. "You wanna dance?"

Volt turned to me, having that same drunken look in his eyes. "Not sure if you could keep up with me, baby."

"Believe me, I've got some serious moves."

"Oh, yeah?" he challenged. "Then let's see these serious moves." He set his whiskey down and guided me onto the dance floor. People were crammed on the tile underneath the sea of stars, and there were only a few more songs left until the wedding was over.

Volt did a fancy spin and pulled me into him like he'd done it a hundred times.

"Whoa...someone used to watch *Dirty Dancing* when they were home from school."

He spun me around again. "Women think dancing is similar to sex. So, I had to make sure I was good in both departments."

"Are you?"

"Maybe you should find out for yourself." He moved his hands as he got into the music, and I was surprised he could loosen up so well. When he wasn't being stiff, he was actually a lot of fun.

"Well, I know that isn't true because I'm a much better dancer than a lover."

"I don't believe that."

"It's true." My filter was off because I'd had way too much to drink. "Maybe that was why Drew was getting around." Now it was easy to talk about it because I was over what happened. It didn't sting anymore.

"Shut up." He pulled me closer to him as we kept dancing. "That's not true. I know for a fact it's not true."

"No, you don't."

"I've kissed you. Believe me, I didn't want to stop. The only reason why I did was because I knew you didn't really want it. But if you did...nothing would have stopped me from having you."

"But I was out of my mind at the time... I don't normally kiss like that."

"So you only do that with me?" he asked quietly.

"I don't know..." I wasn't sure what I was saying anymore. I pulled away from him and started dancing again, trying not to think about anything with too much detail. If I did, I would just get confused.

And I was already confused.

***

We sat together in the back seat while his mom drove back to New York. I was still drunk from all the wine and dancing. When we first got into the car, I was a little sweaty from moving around so much. But I was too tired to care about Volt noticing.

I rested my head on his shoulder while he kept his arm around me. We were snuggled close together, both exhausted and buzzed. I drifted in and out of sleep. Sometimes, the lights from passing cars burned through my eyelids and stirred me. But when the road was dark, I drifted off again. Volt ran his fingers through my hair gently, lulling me back to sleep whenever I was stirred awake.

His mom spoke from the front of the car at some point. "Where to, Volt?"

"My apartment," he answered.

She continued driving for several minutes until we came to a stop. "Good night, baby."

"Good night, Mom."

I forced myself to wake up so I could say goodbye. "It was nice meeting you, Vivian. Thanks for the lift."

"Anytime, sweetheart." She turned around and gave my hand a gentle squeeze.

I was just about to step out of the car when Volt scooped me into his arms and lifted me out. "See you later." He shut the door with his hip and walked to the entryway.

"You don't need to carry me..." I was already drifting again, comfortable in his arms.

"It doesn't seem like you want to walk," he said with a chuckle.

"Well, I know you haven't been to the gym lately, so I'm giving you a workout."

"A workout?" he asked with a laugh. "You don't weigh enough to be a workout." He carried me into the building and then up to his apartment. Once we were inside, he immediately carried me into the bedroom.

I knew I shouldn't be there because Sage had a problem with it. But I really didn't want to walk home, and walking at that time of night when I was still drunk wasn't the best idea anyway.

Volt stripped off his clothes until he was in his boxers before he slid into bed beside me. He spooned me from behind, hooking his arm around my waist and resting his forehead against the back of my neck.

I was so comfortable I dared not move. I was still in my dress, but I was too tired to take it off. His scent enveloped me, making me remember that night in a blur of images. The scruff from his chin brushed against my skin, somehow lulling me into a deep sleep I never wanted to wake from.

I wanted to stay there—forever.

Chapter Five

Volt

We didn't wake up until one the next day.

Taylor's body was wrapped tightly around mine. She was snuggling with me like I was her favorite teddy bear.

I loved seeing her wrapped around me like that. But I knew it was just a fleeting moment. She was there now, but when she woke up, she would leave like she always did. I continued to set myself up for failure, and just when I thought I couldn't get hurt again, I did.

Taylor stretched her arms before she woke up. Her makeup was smeared, and her hair was a mess, but she rocked the look. The only thing missing was red and puckered lips.

And being naked.

"I hate being hung over..." She ran her hand up my chest without even realizing it.

"Yeah, it's a bitch." I grabbed two tablets of painkillers and handed them over.

She swallowed them dry. "Now I'm ready to go back to sleep."

"Good plan." The longer she was in my bed, the better.

"But I'm hungry…"

"You want the chef to make you something?"

"You don't have to cook for me, Volt."

"I don't mind." I never cooked for anyone else, but I'd cook for her. "I say we make some breakfast and watch football all day. No grooming and no clothes."

"No clothes?" she asked with a laugh.

"I mean, no street clothes." *Or just no clothes in general.*

"I can get down with that. This dress is the most uncomfortable thing in the world."

"I have clothes for you."

"That would be much appreciated."

I grabbed a t-shirt and shorts for her to wear, and I pulled on sweatpants so she wouldn't see my hard-on throughout the day. She'd already rubbed it so it probably wasn't necessary, but I would feel more comfortable.

After we had breakfast, we sat on the couch together and watched football all day. This is what I usually did in the fall and winter, but I usually did it alone or with the guys. Never with a girl.

During every commercial, she pulled out her phone and played a game of Candy Crush. This time, she looked

96

too tired, so she set her phone on the coffee table and closed her eyes.

I didn't dare wake her up because she looked too peaceful. She lounged on my couch, looking like a tiny person in my baggy clothes. It was hard to remember a time when I didn't feel this way about her. Before she walked into my heart, I would have started out my morning by saying goodbye to the lover who slept over. Then I would spend my day alone, doing whatever I wanted to do without thinking about anyone else.

And I liked it that way.

But now, everything was different. I wanted to spend all my time with her, and I wanted her to feel the same way about me. It was frustrating to want someone you couldn't have. It was even more frustrating that I couldn't tell her...even though I made a few comments here and there.

Her phone started to vibrate on the coffee table. The screen lit up, and a name appeared on the screen.

Sage.

Why wouldn't this guy just disappear? Why did he have to be good-looking and dreamy? Why did he have to take my girl away?

I glanced at Taylor and noticed she was still asleep. Hopefully, she wouldn't wake up.

Sage's phone call ended, but his name was still on the screen.

I wanted to swipe it away, so she would never know he called.

It would be so easy to do.

She wouldn't call him back and would spend the rest of the day with me.

All I had to do was swipe.

I checked to make sure she was still sleeping before I snatched the phone and held my thumb to the screen. I just wanted to swipe and hide the notification. She would only see it if she went to her missed calls.

Just do it.

I continued to hold the phone, unsure if I could actually go through with it. If I did, I would be the biggest asshole in the world. If she really liked this guy, I couldn't sabotage their relationship. I could linger and hope for my chance to swoop in when they broke up, but I couldn't purposely destroy what they had.

No, I couldn't do that to her.

Despite how shitty it made me feel, I put the phone back.

And left the message untouched.

***

I held up the pie. "Hey, Mom."

Instead of being happy to see me, like she always was, she looked disappointed. "Where's Taylor?"

"She couldn't make it." Because I never asked her. She was probably out with that douchebag.

"Oh... I wanted your father to meet her."

"He'll get his chance."

She just stared at me, totally void of emotion.

"Alright then..." I walked inside and didn't wait for the hug I usually received from my mother. I set the pie on the counter then walked into the dining room. "Hey, Pop. Feeling better?"

"Lots better." He stood up and hugged me, but he definitely looked different. He looked like he lost ten pounds of water. His neck was slender, and his face was hollow. "It's so nice to eat solid food again."

I sat across from him and helped myself to a glass of wine. The food was already set on the table. "Where's Connor?"

"So, I heard you have a lady friend."

Dad wasn't as obsessed with the idea of marriage as Mom, but it was important to him. "Yeah. Her name is Taylor."

"Your mother made it sound like she's the most perfect woman who ever walked the earth."

Pretty damn accurate. "She is."

Dad chuckled. "I'm glad you found someone, and I can't wait to meet her."

"Thanks. I think you'll like her."

"I don't need to like her since your mother already loves her."

Mom joined us at the table and served our plates. Soon, we were eating quietly together. "What are you doing for Thanksgiving?" Mom asked.

"I don't have any plans," I said. "I figured I would come over here."

"Great," Mom said. "Does that mean you'll be bringing Taylor?" She didn't bother playing it cool. Her desperation permeated the air like toxic gas.

"I'll ask." I cut into my chicken and ate quietly. "So, where's Connor?"

"Couldn't make it," Dad said. "Had to work late."

100

My brother and I weren't very close even though we were similar in age. He worked as an attorney for a financial group in Manhattan. He was pretty big time. "Are you back at work, Dad?"

"Yeah," he said. "And the work piled on my shoulders the second I walked in the door. You remember that new teacher I had? Well, the parents are totally fed up with her. There hasn't been a single fieldtrip, her second exam was totally different than the first one and most of the kids got C's. The kids say she's too hard. And that's saying something since these kids are brilliant."

I stopped eating and felt my blood run cold.

"She's being replaced after Christmas. I'm already holding interviews."

Shit. Shit. Shit. "Dad, don't you think you're being a little harsh?"

"No." He kept eating. "You should see the emails that hit my inbox every day. I shouldn't have hired a new teacher. That was my fault, and I'm paying the price."

I had to save Taylor. She was a good teacher in a bad situation. "Dad, don't you think it would be worse for the kids if you replace a teacher halfway through the year?"

"Not if they aren't learning anything," he snapped.

"But they are learning," I argued. "Maybe she's trying a new teaching method."

"Well, it's clearly not working." Dad sipped his wine while he stared at me. "Why do you care about this so much?"

I didn't want them to know it was Taylor. It would ruin her image to my parents. She had to redeem herself first. That was the only way it would work out in her favor. Plus, if she knew the truth, she would throw in the towel altogether. She was giving everything she had, and if that wasn't enough, she'd probably change careers. "Once upon a time, I was a new teacher. I needed some time to learn the ropes, but once I did, I was a great teacher. Instead of kicking her aside, nurture her. Help her. Have you even given her a warning?"

"Well...no." Dad held the glass of wine in his hand.

"Maybe you should talk to her," I suggested. "How is she supposed to fix anything if she doesn't know there's a problem? And stop giving the parents whatever they want. You guys are the teachers, not them."

"I would agree with you if they weren't paying so much money," Dad said.

"Just give this teacher some time. And direction. Don't just pull the plug when she doesn't know there's a problem." That's terrible communication, and even worse, it wasn't very professional.

"Alright. Fine."

At least I diverted that crisis.

"Anyway," Dad said. "What's new with you?"

A lot was new with me. But I couldn't tell them about any of it.

***

I was going on empty at that point.

The situation with Taylor was just getting worse and worse with every passing week. I expected myself to pull away and slowly move on, but that didn't happen. If anything, I held on tighter. She was my *someone*, the person I talked to about mushy crap.

But I couldn't talk to her about this.

Derek and I had been best friends since the beginning of time, but we'd drifted apart lately. After I got my heart broken, I went to the extreme and closed out everyone—until Taylor softened me up again.

Maybe I should talk to him.

He assumed I had feelings for Taylor anyway. Everyone did. He would keep it a secret if I asked him to. I knew he would. So I decided to go for it. I texted him. *Hey, man. What are you doing?*

Just got home. What's up?

Can I come by? I hadn't hung out with him in a while, so it felt strange having this conversation.

Sure. See you soon.

I walked to his place and knocked on the door. He didn't seem to think anything was different between us because he acted exactly the same as always. "Hey, asshole. You want a beer?"

"A big one, cunt."

"Coming right up." He snatched a bottle from the fridge and tossed it to me.

I twisted off the cap and flicked it on the coffee table before I sat on the couch.

He fell onto the other couch and immediately put his feet up. A baseball game was on, and the score didn't favor the Yankees. "What's new with you?"

We made small talk about work and life. He told me he hooked up with a few girls but none of them led to anything promising.

"What about you?" he asked.

This was the moment of truth. "I haven't been with anyone lately."

"Like, since yesterday?"

"Uh, no. More, like, in a month."

He sat upright and gave me a hard expression. "Shit, you have HIV."

That was the last thing I expected him to say. "Dude, no."

"It's okay. It's a treatable disease now. It's not the end of the world."

"Derek, I don't have HIV," I said calmly. It was embarrassing to even be accused of it.

"Then why would you go through a dry spell?"

Because of a woman. "I haven't been interested in it." I kept beating around the bush because it was difficult to admit these feelings out loud.

"Oh shit." He rubbed the back of his neck. "I didn't know..."

Know what?

"When did you come out?"

Now I just wanted to smack him upside the head. "Derek, I'm not gay. I have feelings for Taylor, and I'm not sure what to do about them. I don't have HIV, and I don't like men."

His jaw dropped like that revelation was worse than the first two. He slowly raised his hand and pointed right at me. "I knew it!"

I rolled my eyes.

"I knew you had a thing for her, and you kept telling me I was being a stupid asshole."

"You were being a stupid asshole. And I didn't have feelings for her then." *At least, I don't think I did.*

"It's so obvious. You spend every waking hour with this woman, and if anyone even looks at her, you flip out."

I didn't deny any of that. "You can't tell anyone, alright? I don't want it to get back to her."

"Why wouldn't you want her to know?"

The truth was undeniable. I could try to run from it, but it would just sneak up on me. "She doesn't feel the same way."

"She doesn't?" he asked in surprise. "Are you sure about that?"

I was more sure than he knew. "Yes. Trust me."

"But how would you know unless you've asked her?"

"Dude, I just know. I know when a woman is into me and when she isn't."

"And how do you know with Taylor?"

"Well, she's dating other guys...that's a big clue." Sarcasm dripped from my voice, and I couldn't keep it back. It burned like seeping venom.

"Who's she dating? I thought Drew was out of the picture?"

"She's dating someone else... Some stupid douchebag."

"Why is he a douchebag?" Derek asked. "Why would Taylor date him if he was a douchebag?"

"Well...he's not actually a douchebag." I just hated him because he had the woman I wanted. And he didn't do anything to get her. He just saw her across the room and asked her out. He didn't deserve her more than I did. "I just don't like him."

"I'm gonna need a second to process this... Volt actually has feelings."

"Whatever." I knew I would be teased for this, and I didn't bother fighting it.

"When did this start?"

"Not sure. But a while ago."

"What happened? You just woke up one morning and realized Tayz was awesome?"

"I always knew she was awesome. But no, it didn't happen that way. I'm not sure when these feelings started. I think they began long before I realized they were even there." I think every other piece of me fell for her, but my mind held off the longest. Eventually, that snapped too—like a twig.

"If you aren't going to tell her how you feel, then why are you telling me this?"

Just like everyone else, I needed someone to talk to. I was in a difficult situation, and I had no idea what to do about it. Taylor would have the best advice, but since she was the subject of the problem, she would be a little biased.

And that would be awkward as hell.

"I don't know what to do about it. I guess I'm asking for help."

"You don't know what to do about Tayz?"

I nodded.

"Telling her how you feel is out of the question?"

"Yep."

"Well…I guess you can just wait it out. She has to break up with this new guy eventually, right?"

"That's the problem." I hated what I was about to say. "She really likes this one. She told me she sees it going somewhere and crap like that." Why? Just because he was good-looking? I was good-looking too. I could give her the damn world on a silver platter. "And if she really likes him, I can't mess with it."

"Why not?"

"Because that would make me the biggest dick in the world." I knew if the situation were reversed, she wouldn't do that to me. What kind of friend would I be if I purposely ruined something good just so I could have what I wanted? If I really did that, I wouldn't deserve her.

"When did you start caring about being a dick?"

"Since I met Taylor." She smoothed my edges and healed my cuts. She brought back the goodness in me, the part of me I thought had disappeared forever.

"Wow." His joking nature had disappeared. "So you've really got it bad, huh?"

I shrugged. "It sucks. I hate it."

"I don't understand how she doesn't know. I mean, it's obvious to the rest of us."

"When we first met, I didn't show much interest in her. She must think first impressions are forever and my feelings would never change. That's my only explanation. Because you're right, it's painfully obvious."

"Beautiful but sad…"

I shot him a glare.

"I mean that in a good way," he said quickly.

"Yeah, you better."

"So…what now?"

"I don't know… What do you think I should do?"

He laughed. "You think I'm a good person to ask?"

"You're my best friend, right?"

His chuckles died away. "Dude, we both know I'm not your best friend anymore. Taylor is."

"But—"

"I'm okay with that. That's how it should be." He gave me a slight look of affection. "I just hope she realizes how she feels eventually."

"Realizes?"

"I think she feels the same way. She's stuck to you like glue."

"I don't think she does… It doesn't seem like it."

"You're right. It doesn't seem like it. But I think she does. She just doesn't know. Just how you felt however long ago."

"Like, subconsciously?"

He nodded. "She has to. A guy and a girl are never that close and platonic unless one of them is gay. And since we already had the conversation about you being gay, that would mean she was the gay one. But since she's seeing some guy, that can't be true."

I rolled my eyes when I thought of that conversation.

"So, yeah. I guess you can just wait it out."

"How long?"

"I don't know," he said with a shrug.

"What if he's around for a long time?"

He drank his beer as he considered my question. "Then you probably should try to move on. I mean, are you really going to wait around for a year? Maybe more? That would be unrealistic."

"I know."

"If you don't see this happening, maybe you should try to get over her."

But how was that possible? "I don't know if I can."

"Stop sleeping around and start dating. Have actual relationships with people. And stop spending so much time with Taylor."

Both of those were equally hard. "I don't know..."

111

"If you don't, you're going to stay in this vortex forever."

I didn't want that. It was unbearable. "You're right."

"So, you're officially moving on?"

I couldn't keep getting sucked in over and over. "When Taylor spends the night at my place, I fall harder for her. When she wears my clothes and sleeps next to me, I die a little inside. And then when I watch her leave to be with whatever-the-fuck-his-name is, I'm crushed. Every day is more agonizing than the previous one. And it makes me into a person I don't like. I almost hid a missed call from the guy from Taylor. I always make little jabs about the fact she should be with me instead of him. I don't like who I've become…"

Derek was about to take a drink when he lowered his beer instead. "She sleeps with you?"

"Sometimes."

"And she still wants to be with him?"

I nodded.

"Man…you really need some space."

"You're right."

"It's definitely time to take a step back. Because if she's sleeping with you but still wanting to be with someone else, you're screwed. I'm sorry, but that's just not normal. I would never just sleep with Taylor like it was no big deal."

"I know." It was the weirdest shit ever.

"You'll get through it, man. I'm here for you."

Thankfully, I had him to talk to. "I know."

Chapter Six

Taylor

"Everyone, take a seat. No phones."

The students filed into the auditorium and took their seats. Their conversations filled the small room, and most of them were teasing each other about one thing or another. The presentation was about to start on the massive screen projected directly overhead.

"Now *we* get a break." Volt stood next to me off to the side. We leaned against the wall and stood near the stairway. None of the students could slip out while we were manning the exit.

"Thank goodness. I knew this field trip would be work, but I didn't realize just how much work. I'm so glad you're here." That was an understatement. Volt was a godsend. He had a natural way with kids and got them to listen without having to exert his authority. The students automatically looked up to him, probably because he was confident and successful.

"I'm glad I could help." His hands were in the pockets of his suit, and he kept a foot of space between us. We hadn't spoken since the morning after the wedding, and something didn't feel right. He was much more quiet than usual and even a little cold.

"Everything alright?"

"Yeah. Just tired. I haven't been exhausted like this since my last year of teaching."

"Do you miss it?"

"Sometimes," he answered. "Right now? No."

I chuckled. "This is why I've been dreading the field trip. I knew it would be difficult."

"It gets easier as you go along. And the students will remember this forever. That's why field trips are so important."

"So I'm making their memories?"

"That's a good description."

The theatre darkened, and the presentation began. The projector showed the different stars in the sky and gave a history of the universe. When the students were quiet, I knew they were interested.

The presentation lasted forty-five minutes before it came to an end. The lights came back on, and the students jumped out of their seats.

"Break time is over," Volt said with a sigh. "Let's round them up."

I felt like a sheep dog, and these were my sheep. "Alright. Let's go." We got the kids out of the auditorium and through the rest of the museum. The place had a living rain forest that was isolated from the rest of the building. Even the humidity and temperature were different.

The kids loved that part of the exhibit even more than the planetarium. They pointed at the lizards and parrots hanging from the branches. Butterflies floated around, their wings different colors.

"This place is really cool." Volt walked beside me at the rear of the line. The twelve students were in front of us, constantly in our line of sight. "A little warm to be wearing a suit, but very cool."

"I love it here. I've never seen so many butterflies."

"And look how big they are." Volt stopped at the edge of the barrier and looked under the forest canopy. "I've never seen butterflies that big in my life."

"Because they don't visit New York often."

He chuckled. "Yeah, I guess so."

A large white butterfly fluttered through the air. She flapped her large wings and aimed right for Volt.

"She's coming right for us," I whispered.

"I know... Don't move."

The butterfly landed on Volt's shoulder. She continued to flap her wings but remained stationary.

"Aww! You're so lucky."

Volt watched it from his peripheral vision. "I must look like a tree. Thanks...I think."

I took a picture with my phone. "I'll have to show this to your mother."

"She'd love that."

The butterfly took flight again and drifted back into the canopy.

"I think she liked you."

"I've always been a bit of a ladies man," he said with a smile. "I guess that applies to insects too."

"Very pretty insects."

He turned back to the line and realized our students were gone. "It looks like we lost them."

I may be a new teacher, but I wasn't totally clueless. "No. They lost us."

***

The fieldtrip finally ended when the parents collected all of their students. They left the campus and returned home, gone so I wouldn't have to see them again until Monday.

Thankfully.

Volt stood beside me on the sidewalk. "I think that was a success."

"Now that it's over."

"No, it was good. The students learned a lot and had a good time. That's your goal—and you succeeded."

"Thanks for being a chaperone. If I had to do this with one of the parents... Yikes."

"Yeah, they can be clingy." Now that we were outside, it was chilly. His breath escaped his mouth in the form of vapor. He looked up into the trees, and the light from the streetlamp highlighted his face. After a few seconds, he turned back to me. "Well, enjoy your break until the next one."

"I will." It was past dinnertime, and I was starving. "Want to get something to eat?"

His face lit up like he was immediately going to say yes, but that look instantly disappeared. He closed his mouth tightly then looked at his watch. "You know, I should probably get home. My mom dropped off dinner earlier today, and I should eat it. Somehow, she knows if I don't."

I waited for him to invite me over.

But all I heard was crickets.

"I'll see you around." Volt raised his hand and held it up.

I eyed it, unsure what he was doing. "What?"

"High-five?" He moved his hand slightly. "You know what that is, right?"

"Oh." I returned the high-five and realized we'd never done that before.

"See ya." He walked away with his hands in his pockets. Not once did he look back or give me a wave. He didn't even offer to walk me home like he usually did. Something was out of place, but I couldn't put my finger on it.

Was I just overthinking things? Was I seeing something that wasn't there at all?

Knowing I was looking too much into it, I turned the opposite way and walked to my apartment. My instincts were usually right, and when something was out of place, I knew it.

But this time, I wasn't sure.

Chapter Seven

Volt

I went on a lot of dates.

I picked up women from all over the place. Sometimes the bar, sometimes the subway, and sometimes from a dating app. Manhattan was the homeland of some of the most gorgeous women on the planet, and I was lucky enough to encounter them in their natural habitat.

But none of them did anything for me.

At the end of the dates, I knew the relationships wouldn't go any further. So I walked them to their doors and said goodnight. But when sex was off the table, and I didn't make a move for even a kiss, they wanted me more. They gave me their best moves and tried to seduce me into coming inside their apartments.

But I never took the bait.

What the hell was wrong with me?

My sex drive was completely non-existent. The women were sexy in every way imaginable, but I didn't even get hard. They had beautiful faces and full lips, but my mouth never ached to kiss them.

All I could think about was Taylor.

I was seriously screwed.

"How's the dating going?" Derek asked across the table. We were having drinks at one of our regular bars. A sea of people surrounded us, blending into the shadows of the dark room. It was just him and I, the rest of the gang staying in.

"Fucking terrible."

"You haven't been out with anyone?" He drank his beer then cracked a few nuts from the bowl on the table.

"I've been out with *everyone*." I'd dated models, ice skaters, news anchors, everyone.

"And you didn't like any of them?" he asked incredulously.

"Something is wrong with me. There was nothing wrong with any of those women. They were all beautiful and sexy... I just didn't care for them. At the end of the date, I would say goodnight and leave, but that just made them want to sleep with me more. In fact, I get more action from not trying than when I actually try." It was a crazy paradox.

"Every guy in the world wishes they had that problem."

"Everyone except me."

"So...no second dates?"

I shook my head.

"How many dates are we talking?"

I shrugged. "I don't know… Seven?"

"You went out with seven different women this week?" he asked in surprise. "That's a different chick every night."

"Sometimes I had two dates on the same night." So it wasn't every single night.

He rolled his eyes. "That's incredible."

"Not really. You could get as many dates if you tried."

He laughed sarcastically. "Uh, no. Not everyone can pull that off."

"You can if you have the confidence."

"Whatever, man. You're a pretty boy, and we both know it."

"I'm not a pretty boy," I argued. "I'm just a man."

"Sure." He drank his beer and scoped out the people in the bar. "So now what?"

"Meaning?"

"Are you going to keep doing this?" He eyed a brunette in the corner. Only half of his brain seemed to be in the conversation.

"I don't know." The idea seemed tortuous. Anytime I was sitting across from a woman at dinner, I kept comparing her to Taylor. They weren't funny or goofy like Taylor. And they never seemed to understand my humor. In fact, it just made me realize how incredible Taylor was. And it made me hate myself more. If I just made a move when I had the chance, things might have been different.

But I was too stupid to say anything.

"You can't throw in the towel."

"But I can't keep doing this."

"I don't think you're keeping an open mind."

He hit the nail right on the head. "Because I don't want to. I know who I want to be with."

He pulled his gaze away from the brunette and turned his focus on me. When he narrowed his eyes and remained silent for nearly a minute, I knew something irritating was going to fly out of his mouth. "Are you in love with her?"

That word went straight to my stomach and made me feel sick. "No."

"Are you sure about that?" he pressed. "Because that's how you sound."

"I'm not in love with her." I may like her, and I may be obsessed with her. But I couldn't be in love with someone when I wasn't even in a relationship. I wasn't sure if I could ever be in love at all. After my heart was broken, I was never the same. I trusted Taylor more than anyone on this earth, but I didn't trust her not to hurt me. She was hurting me right that second.

"I don't believe you."

"That's funny because I don't care."

Derek gave me a hard look. "If you are, which I think you are, maybe you should just tell her. If you just liked her, that would be one thing. But if you're head over heels in love with her, then that's a different story."

"Not in love with her."

"And you're sure?"

"Absolutely."

"Because you were sure you didn't like her..."

I avoided his gaze. "I'm sure."

"Alright." He finally backed off. "There's this cool chick from my work. Maybe I can set you up with her."

"I don't need to be set up." I could get my own dates. I could get a ton of dates.

"Clearly, you do. I'm telling you that I already know this woman is cool. So you won't be getting a dull person."

"If she's so cool, why haven't you dated her?"

"Believe me, I tried."

I wish I could go back to a time when Taylor was just some woman. I remembered spotting her on the street while she was trying to decipher a map of the city. There were no feelings on my part, and I missed that emptiness. Why couldn't I wipe her from my brain and start over?

"I swear she's really cool. Sexy too."

"Cool like Taylor? Sexy like Taylor?"

"Definitely."

I had nothing to lose, so I decided to go for it. "I'll give it a shot."

He clanked his beer against mine. "Excellent."

***

Julia turned out to be pretty cool. She was a computer programmer for Derek's company, and she was a cyclist on the side. She competed in bicycle century races around the nation, and apparently, she was pretty good at them. She was pretty too.

But I still didn't feel anything.

At dinner, I found myself thinking about Taylor and wondering what she was doing at that very moment. We hadn't talked much that week, and whenever she texted me, I always gave her short answers. I avoided seeing her at all costs, and whenever she asked if I wanted to get lunch or dinner, I told her I was busy.

She didn't deserve my distance, not when she'd always been a good friend to me. But I had to work on me. If I saw her all the time, I would never get better. I would never see Julia as the awesome woman she was because I'd keep thinking about the woman I couldn't have.

Despite how difficult it was, I knew I was doing the right thing.

And now I had to keep doing it.

I went out with Julia twice, and we had a good time, but I never made a move to kiss her or do anything else. The idea of kissing her felt oddly strange. It seemed like a betrayal to Taylor, which made even less sense.

But then again, nothing made sense anymore.

Chapter Eight

Taylor

When the school day was over, the principal walked into my office.

Principal Rosenthal and I hadn't had too many conversations over the course of my time at Bristol Academy. He was the person who hired me, but after that, we didn't see each other much. He was busy running the school, and I was busy running my classroom.

"Hello, Principal Rosenthal." I stacked up my papers on my desk and turned off my computer screen. "What brings you here?"

He shut the door behind him and approached my desk, his hands in his pockets. He had crystal blue eyes that were both comforting and terrifying. His strong jaw had some gray hair, and the features of his face reminded me of someone, but I couldn't think of whom.

His silence was unnerving. Normally when I saw him, he was talkative and warm. Right now, he was a different man. I felt like a child being disciplined for a crime I didn't know I committed.

"Hello, Ms. Thomas." He leaned against one of the student's desks and faced me, his arms across his chest. "Are you free right now?"

"Yeah. Just packing up my things." I abandoned the papers on the desk because I knew this conversation was serious. I didn't do anything wrong, but I couldn't help but feel like I had.

"So...I've been getting a lot of feedback from the parents."

I knew this conversation would be a terrible one. "Oh?"

"And I took a look at your last two exams. It seemed like the students did well on the first one, but not the second."

"Well, I felt like the first one was too easy."

"Maybe," he said. "But some of our brightest students got B's and C's on that last exam. These are the kind of kids that are fast-tracked to Brown and Columbia. They don't get B's and C's."

My defensive side immediately flared, but I kept my attitude in line. "Well, they didn't do the work. I feel like these kids think they can slide by based on who they are or who their families are. That test was challenging but fair. I think they learned a great deal, and they'll be better prepared for exams in the future."

"I understand what you're trying to do. Really. Challenging young minds prepares them for the real world. But I have some concerned parents that are afraid these B's and C's are going to affect their college admissions. And frankly, they will."

That attitude was building up even more. "You want me to just hand out good grades?"

"That's not what I'm saying," he said quickly. "But I think this exam was too challenging for juniors."

"They're almost in college. They should be challenged."

"And that's what classroom time is for. But when I looked at the exam, the questions were purposely worded to confuse the students."

"And what do you think the SAT does?" Now my anger was in full force, and I couldn't keep it back. When I agreed to teach the brightest minds at a private school, I expected to have the brightest kids in the nation. I expected to push them to levels they'd never been pushed to before. I expected to give them an edge other students wouldn't receive.

Principal Rosenthal cleared his throat and rubbed his chin. "Ms. Thomas, I hired you because I thought you were qualified for the job. I still think you are. But you've lost your perspective in this matter. You're invested in these kids, which is a good thing. But you aren't approaching this in the right way."

"I'm doing my best to prepare these kids for the real world. How can I do that when I'm being hindered all the time?"

"You know what kind of lesson plans to make. You know what kind of exams to write. Just stick with the protocol."

"But—"

"I intend to replace you after the Christmas break."

My jaw hung open, and unsuspecting pain stabbed me right in the heart. I lost my breath because I was so winded. My mind fell into a spin, and I couldn't think straight.

"This is your only warning. If things don't turn around, you'll be asked to leave Bristol Academy."

I still couldn't speak. Never in my life had I been fired. I really was just trying to do the right thing. My students were most important to me. I wanted them to get into the best colleges and succeed in life. I never wanted them to struggle. And I wanted them to thank me for it one day.

"The parents are jumping down my throat over these poor grades. They aren't going to stop until something is done. Not only do you have to impress me, but you have to impress them. Good luck." He turned away and walked out of my classroom. His feet sounded on the tile and echoed down the hall. The sound continued until he was so far away there wasn't a single noise.

And then I was alone.

***

I managed to get home without shedding a single tear. My chest ached from the difficulty of breathing. My tongue was dry, but my eyes were wet. I felt sick to my stomach but dead at the same time.

And I felt numb.

Without thinking about it, I collapsed onto the couch and pulled out my phone. The movements were so fluid they were mindless. My mind and body were one as they worked together.

I called the first person that came to mind. I listened to the phone ring over and over and waited for his voice to pick up on the receiver. His words always soothed me no matter how upset I was. He knew the right thing to say in any situation.

Because he was my best friend.

But it went to voicemail.

I'd never gotten his voicemail before. There was never a time when he didn't take my call. It made me wonder if he lost his phone, or he was in the shower. There was no other explanation for it.

I sent him a text message. *Call me when you get a chance. It's important.* I set my phone on the coffee table and replayed everything that happened with the principal. My pain came from the frustration of being treated so unfairly. I was doing my best to give these students what they needed, but all the parents cared about were the grades. They didn't get good grades because they didn't earn them. It was as simple as that.

My eyes became wetter.

My chest ached with every breath.

I refused to cry. It was stupid and pointless. All it did was show weakness.

But I couldn't help it. I was heartbroken.

Volt called me back almost instantly. The second the message formed on his screen, he reached out to me.

I answered the phone and tried to keep my voice steady. "Hey."

"Hey, what's up?" he asked with his usual deep voice. "You alright?"

"Yeah..." I fingered a piece of twine that came loose from one of the couch pillows. I wrapped it around my finger over and over, trying to concentrate on what I was doing and not what I was feeling.

His voice softened when he heard my heartbreak. "It doesn't sound like it."

"Do you think you could come over?"

"Uh..." His voice faded for a moment, and that's when I recognized the sounds of conversations in the background. He seemed to be inside a restaurant. "Yeah, I'll be there soon."

`"Thank you."

"Of course."

***

He walked inside my apartment without knocking and joined me on the couch. When he saw the tears in my eyes, he cupped my cheeks and wiped the moisture away

135

with the pads of his thumbs. Instead of asking me millions of questions, he just stared at me, the same heartbreak I felt was written all over his face.

I wanted to tell him everything, but I couldn't get anything out. Saying it out loud would just make me feel worse.

He ran his fingers through my hair then pulled me close to him. His chest was more comfortable than any bed I'd ever slept on, and his warmth gave me some form of peace. "Did you and Sage break up?" Instead of sounding as depressed as he had a moment ago, he sounded different, maybe even hopeful.

"No..." I hadn't thought about him once since I received the horrible news.

Volt's hands paused on my cheeks, and his flinch told me he hadn't been expecting that answer. He slowly pulled his hands away and returned them to his thighs, no longer touching me at all.

And that made me feel worse.

He looked down, his eyes narrowed and his lips pressed tightly together. He cleared his throat before he looked at me again. "Then what's wrong? What happened?"

"I lost my job."

Volt froze as he stared at me, unable to process what I said. It took him nearly half a minute to react. "What?"

"The principal came in and said I wasn't doing my job. Too many of the kids performed poorly on the exam, and apparently, these kinds of kids don't get grades like that. He said he'll replace me after Christmas if I don't turn things around."

"Then you didn't lose your job." His face was pale, like the blow hurt him as much as it hurt me.

"No. But I'm quitting."

"You can't quit, Taylor."

"Yes, I can. Maybe I'm not cut out to be a teacher. Maybe this was all a mistake."

"That's not true," he said quietly. "This has nothing to do with you."

"It has everything to do with me."

"Listen to me." He grabbed my hand and held it in his. Our fingers were intertwined, and I could feel his pulse through his skin. "Private schools like Bristol are different than the system you've been taught. They run on different rules and standards. It has nothing to do with your teaching abilities."

"I just tried to challenge them. I tried to prepare them."

"And there is nothing wrong with that. But in the private district, things are a lot more controlled. This isn't a reflection on you. That place is so political it'll make your head explode. Why do you think I opened a tutoring program? Because there are better ways of teaching kids than the school system will allow you to believe."

I heard what he said, but I didn't really listen to it. "You were right, Volt. I should have listened to you."

"That's not true—"

"Yes, it is. And we both know it."

He gave me a sad look, like he'd give anything to be wrong. "Quitting isn't the answer."

"I can't go back there."

"It'll look terrible on your resume if you do that. At least finish out the school year."

"I won't make it past Christmas anyway."

"That's not true."

"Yes, it is. He said he's already looking to replace me."

"If you do exactly what he asks, that won't happen. I know you're upset right now, but quitting isn't the answer. You're going to turn all of this around."

Maybe I could. Maybe I couldn't. "I don't care enough to turn things around. I'll just get a job in a lab somewhere."

"But you won't be happy doing that. Taylor, I've seen you with your kids. You care about them."

"Of course I do. I love them." Even the annoying ones that never listened to me. They were all unique in their own ways, but they were also wonderful in their own ways. I wanted the best for them—always.

"Then don't give up."

"I'm not going back to work at a place where I'm being micromanaged. They're going to watch every little thing I do, and that's just going to make me flustered."

"It'll be irritating, but I know you can do it."

"It's not about *can*, Volt. It's about *want*."

He squeezed my hand then leaned forward, forcing himself into my line of sight. "I don't think you'd be crying if you didn't care. I don't think you'd be worked up if it wasn't something you wanted."

He had me there, and I knew it. I gave my kids everything, and the fact none of it meant anything made me feel defeated. I was working for a paycheck just like everyone else. There was nothing else meaningful that went along with it.

It made me feel worthless.

"Baby, listen to me." He grabbed my chin and forced me to look at him. "It's okay to be upset and have a good cry. But it's not okay to give up. You can do this. I know you can."

"But I'm never going to be happy there. Even if I turn everything around, I'll still be the teacher who almost got fired."

"Then get a job somewhere else. But finish out the year."

I wasn't sure if I could come face-to-face with the principal again. He did what he was supposed to do for the school and his teachers, but it still made me sick inside. Bristol Academy used to be my home. Now it felt like a prison.

"Taylor?"

My eyes drifted back to his face.

"You're going to do this. I'll help you."

"Can I just work for your company? I can be an awesome tutor."

He smiled like that idea was tempting. "I'd love that. But you're meant to be a teacher, not a tutor."

"But there's no politics. No bullshit."

"I don't know… I would be your boss."

"You seem like a cool boss to me."

"The grass is always greener on the other side."

I wiped my remaining tears with my forearm. My makeup was running, but there was nothing I could do about it. Volt had already seen me at my worst. "Thanks for coming by."

"Sure. You know I'm always here for you."

"I hope I didn't interrupt anything. It sounded like you were out." I didn't ask what he was doing since we hadn't seen each other much. Whenever we texted each other, he didn't have long responses. And when I asked if he wanted to hang out, he was always busy.

"Yeah, I was. But it's not a big deal."

"Out with the guys?"

"Uh, no. Actually, I'm seeing someone."

Even though that wasn't what I expected him to say, I wasn't surprised. It explained his distance. He wasn't hanging out with me because he was spending time with someone else. His dry spell must be over. "Another booty call to add to the list?"

"Not really." He released my hand. "We've gone out a few times. I'm seeing where it goes."

He was actually dating someone? Like, in the hope it would be a relationship? From what he told me, it seemed like he was incapable of that. In fact, just a few weeks ago, he asked me to pretend to be his girlfriend just to get his parents off his back.

And now he was seeing someone?

When we first met, I felt the attraction to Volt. He was the most handsome man I'd ever seen, and I found myself thinking about him in both romantic and sexual scenarios. But when it was clear he was unattainable, just some kind of playboy, I was forced to look at him differently. Instead of being a potential lover, he became a friend. And that's all he'd ever been.

But it still bothered me.

"Then you must really like her." My job was no longer my concern. I didn't care about it anymore, and it seemed so insignificant in comparison.

"She's pretty cool, I guess." He rested his elbows on his knees and stared at the floor.

"Where did you meet her?"

"Derek introduced us. Thought we would hit it off."

"And have you?"

He nodded. "I guess you could say that."

It was none of my business, and I shouldn't say anything, but I couldn't help it. "I thought you didn't do the relationship thing...and never wanted to?"

He shrugged. "I guess I've become more open-minded to it."

My heart was beating fast. It actually hurt with every thump. "Good for you."

"Being around Clay makes me want to have kids of my own someday. Kinda need a wife to do that."

So he thought about marriage? Like night and day, he turned into a completely different person. I wasn't sure if he was the same man I met six months ago. He was thinking about marriage and a family...something he swore he would never want for the rest of his life.

What changed?

"I'm happy for you." My voice cracked as I spoke, probably the aftermath of crying earlier. "I'd love to meet her."

"Maybe we could go on a double date or something." He leaned back against the couch and crossed his arms over his chest.

"We should. Are you busy on Saturday?" Now that I knew he was into this woman, I had to meet her for myself. I wanted to know what Volt wanted in a woman. Up until that point, it'd only been supermodels for a one-night stay. What was so incredible about this woman that she changed his view on everything?

He flinched at the response, as if he wasn't prepared for my agreement. "You want to go on a double date?"

"Why not? You always meet the men I date. Shouldn't I meet the woman of your dreams?"

He held my gaze. "She's not the woman of my dreams."

"She must be. What else could get you to be monogamous?" Volt was in denial of his feelings most of the time, but now he seemed to realize them. "I told you when you met the right girl, your entire life would change. She'll make you into a different man—but in a good way. I told you so."

"I'm just dating her. I never said I was in love with her."

"But you don't date, remember?"

He sighed in irritation. "Look, I'm trying this dating thing. That doesn't mean I'm going to marry this woman. It just means...what it means."

"I guess I'll see what you're talking about on Saturday."

He sighed again and turned away.

The day turned out to be far worse than I imagined. I might lose my job, and Volt was looking for something serious with a woman. It bothered me in a way I could never explain. I didn't have feelings for him anymore, but I did at one point. I'd fantasized about those lips all over my body. I pictured my fingers running through his hair. The fact we were such good friends and he never considered me as a possible girlfriend was hurtful.

But I should get over it.

He never saw me the way I saw him. To him, I was always that weird girl who got lost in the city. I was that teacher that dressed like a hippie. I was that friend he could turn to for everything—and that's all.

"You should go back to your date. If I'd known, I wouldn't have bothered you." I pulled my knees to my chest and closed off from him, feeling embarrassed that I called when I shouldn't have.

"You never bother me, Taylor."

"You're just saying that...and I appreciate it."

He scooted closer to me on the couch and wrapped his arm around my shoulders. "You know I'm not." He pulled me to his side and rested my head on his shoulder. "My place is right here—next to you."

His closeness felt so nice that I could finally breathe easily. I didn't think about work and all the headaches associated with it. All I cared about was that moment and how safe I felt. Volt chased away my pain like magic. He always knew the right thing to say and when to say it.

I linked my arm through his and listened to his shallow breathing. The blank TV faced us, and I could see our reflection in the screen. His head rested against mine, and his t-shirt clung to his muscled shoulders and powerful chest. His chin was smooth like he shaved that evening and his usual scent washed over me like the smell of my favorite candle.

I wanted to stay like that forever.

Time seemed to stop when we were together. Nothing from the outside world could penetrate us. It was just him and I against everything else. We understood each other on an innate level, better than any other relationship I've ever had.

"Taylor?" His deep voice resonated in my ear, making me feel at peace.

"Yeah?"

He turned his head slightly so he could watch my expression. His breaths fell on my skin, warm and inviting. "Why didn't you call Sage?"

His question hung unanswered in the air. I heard what he said but didn't understand why he said it. "What do you mean?"

"Why did you call me instead of him?"

"I don't know. I wasn't thinking." When I was upset, my instincts just kicked in. My body worked on its own and did whatever was necessary to survive. Volt was the first person that popped into my head. It wasn't Sage, and it wasn't Sara. It was only him. "Why?"

He was silent, not moving and hardly breathing. He finally brushed his face against mine, turning his attention to the blank screen in front of us. Our eyes met in the reflection, and they remained there. "No reason."

***

Sage and I sat side by side at the restaurant. Volt and his date weren't there yet, so we sat together in tense silence. Sage wasn't himself that evening. He didn't say much, and when I asked him a question, he had even less to say.

The basket of bread sat on the table, but neither one of us reached for a bite. The butter was soft, and the cheese had just been grated. Two glasses of red wine had been poured, but neither one of us reached for them.

"Everything okay?" he asked.

I kept searching for them through the windows, wanting to know what Julia looked like. Was she a blonde? A brunette? Possibly a redhead? "Yeah, I'm fine."

"Seem nervous."

"Just tired." And out of place. I wasn't sure why I was so nervous to meet Volt's girlfriend. I'd met new people before. This shouldn't be a big deal.

"Whose idea was it to have a double date?"

"His." But I pressed it.

"Kinda weird but whatever."

"Why is that weird?" I tore my gaze from the window and looked at him.

He drank his wine to cover his unease before he returned the glass to the table. "Never mind."

"You can tell me."

He straightened in his chair like I might give him a bad response. "I think he's into you, and this is just a complex way of pretending he's not."

Sage had never really dropped his suspicion of Volt. "Why is it so hard to believe we're just friends?"

"Because neither one of you are gay."

"You really need to let this go."

"There's nothing to let go," he said calmly. "I still believe he has a thing for you. You can believe what you want, but I know what I see. I'm not jealous or angry. But I'm not stupid either. Maybe one day you'll realize it. Maybe not."

"If Volt had feelings for me, he would have said something a long time ago."

Sage didn't respond, telling me the conversation was over. "How was work this week?"

"It was okay..." I told him about my day from hell a few days ago, and he comforted me just the way Volt did.

"It'll get better. Just keep pushing through."

"Easier said than done."

"It'll be fine in the end. It always is."

"How was your week?"

"Pretty good," he answered. "The Yankees won, so everything is right in the world."

I chuckled. "It's a pretty simple world you live in."

He shrugged. "I like simple."

Volt walked into the restaurant, and my head immediately snapped in his direction. A woman was with him, and I wasn't prepared for how she would look. She was a tall brunette, nearly as tall as he was. She wore a long skirt and a top that showed some of her flat stomach. She had dark skin like she was exotic, and her brown hair was long and shiny. She had sparkling eyes and a perfect smile. Without any further information, I knew this woman was a model.

No doubt about it.

She and Volt approached our table, and it took me a second to realize I needed to stand up. I lost my footing and couldn't really think. Her beauty forced me to take a step back.

Sage immediately turned his gaze on her, and he stared at her longer than necessary.

I wanted to be mad, but I couldn't blame him. She really was gorgeous.

Volt turned to Sage, and their mutual dislike rang in the air. He held up his hand for a handshake. "Nice to see you again."

"Likewise." Sage shook his hand quickly before letting go.

Now I felt stupid wearing an old dress and sandals. My hair was straight, because I didn't have time to do it. I was a plain blob in comparison to this unique woman. I really wished I could stop comparing myself to her. I never did that sort of thing before.

Volt turned to me but didn't touch me. "Hey."

"Hey." My usual enthusiasm died in my throat. For some reason, I didn't want to see him. I actually felt awkward.

He turned to his date and introduced her. "This is Julia."

"Hi, Julia." Sage stepped forward and shook her hand much longer than he shook Volt's. He quickly cleared his throat and stepped back, looking at the ground and the people in the restaurant.

"Hi. It's a pleasure to meet you." I shook her hand next, feeling more hideous the closer I came to her.

"You too." She had a Spanish accent. I couldn't determine exactly what dialect it was. It definitely wasn't regular Spanish. It seemed more South American. "Volt has told me so much about you."

"I hope he said good things," I said with a chuckle.

"For the most part," Volt said. "But a lot of bad things too." He winked at me.

That made me feel better—but only for a second.

We sat down and browsed through our menus. Volt sat directly across from me, and I kept glancing up to watch what he was doing. I wondered where his hands were and if they were to himself.

Julia moved her hand to his thigh under the table. "What are you getting?"

"Not sure," he answered. "How about you?"

Sage kept staring at her. When he took a sip of his wine, he spilled some on his shirt.

That's when I noticed everyone in the restaurant was staring at her.

Volt looked up, and our eyes met. Like he didn't want to be caught staring at me, he quickly looked away.

Maybe this double date thing wasn't such a good idea.

***

Julia had her arm hooked through his as they walked outside together. She clung to him like glue. She whispered words only he could hear, and then she would chuckle at his reaction.

We faced each other on the sidewalk and prepared to say goodnight.

"Well, it was nice meeting all of you." She pressed her tits against his arm because she was tucked into his side so tightly.

"You too," I said with a smile.

"Yeah…" Sage rubbed the back of his neck and cleared his throat.

"Well, have a good night." I didn't have a chance to talk with Volt one-on-one, and I suspected I wouldn't get the opportunity.

"You too." Volt turned away with Julia still on his arm. They walked off together and disappeared into the crowd.

I turned to Sage and felt him grab my hand. "You still think he's just dating her so I won't think he's into me?" Any man could take one look at her and know she was out of this world. I'd never seen a person so beautiful other than people on TV.

He chuckled. "Not anymore."

Chapter Nine

Volt

Julia never dropped my hand. She squeezed it the entire walk to her apartment. I felt her press against me harder and harder, practically climbing on me. Her desire was hot enough to burn through my skin and shoot directly to my blood.

Shit was about to go down.

I walked her to her apartment with the intention of giving her a friendly hug as a goodbye, but she clearly had something else on her mind. She wrapped her arms around my neck then leaned in and gave me a slow kiss.

I liked the kiss. She knew how to move her mouth and make a man crumble. But it was nothing like what I had with Taylor. Our kisses were so strong they bruised our mouths. The heat between us was enough to burn down a swamp. I'd been with so many women in my lifetime, but it only took one special one to completely turn my world upside down.

And this woman wasn't her.

I broke the kiss before it escalated into something more. Julia was a great person, and every guy in the world hated me in that moment. And with what I was about to do, they would all think I was an idiot too. "Thanks for having dinner with me."

She stared at me with the same hungry expression. "Come inside." Her forwardness was sexy because it wasn't desperate. We'd been out a few times and she never made a move like this. She was truly ready.

But I wasn't.

If I went to bed with her, I would think about someone else. And that would be a huge dick move. I couldn't be with one woman while pretending it was someone else. And I couldn't get Taylor out of my mind no matter how hard I tried. Getting to know Julie was supposed to make me forget about her. Somehow, it made me want her more. "I'm flattered, but I don't think that's a good idea." I should just end this now before things get too deep.

"Why not?" She kept her arms around my neck, locking me in place.

"I just..." It would be even worse if I told her the truth. "I won't call you again. And that wouldn't be fair to you."

Instead of being hurt by that, she looked me right in the eye. This woman was fierce in her confidence. "It's her, isn't it?"

"It's who?"

"Taylor."

Shit, did I make my feelings that obvious to someone I'd only known for a few weeks? "I don't know what you mean."

"Yes, you do." Instead of pulling out her claws, she smiled. "I saw the way you looked at her. I can tell there's something there."

Since I'd been caught, I refused to lie. "I've been trying to get over her. Nothing has worked."

"Why are you trying to get over her?"

"Because I can't be with her."

"Who says you can't? If you want something, just take it."

"In case you didn't notice, she's seeing someone." I wished I'd met Julia first. I loved her killer attitude and her simple view of the world. When she wanted something she just took it—like right now. She was beautiful and smart, and she excelled in every other category. If we met before

Taylor walked into my life, maybe things would have been different.

"Then make her stop seeing him."

"Like, break them up?"

She shrugged. "You've got to do what you've got to do, right?"

"No. That's not me."

"You aren't a fighter?" she asked.

"She really likes him. I'm not going to break them up and take away something that makes her happy. Not my style."

"Does she know how you feel?"

I shook my head.

"Then it's time for you to move forward."

"I tried...but failed."

"No, you haven't really tried." She pulled out her keys and got her apartment unlocked. She leaned against the door with a sexy grin on her face. Then she held up her finger and beckoned me inside.

I stayed on the other side of the door.

"I'll make you forget about her, Volt."

"I don't know about that..." Taylor was permanently ingrained in my body. She was like a scar that just wouldn't fade away. There was no possibility of us, and I needed to let it go. But every time I tried, I just held on tighter. "What do you get out of it?"

"A killer orgasm, I would hope." She smiled then pulled me inside her apartment.

"I can do that. But I can't sleep with someone while thinking about someone else. And that's exactly what will happen."

"I'm okay with that." She grabbed my hand and pulled me into her bedroom. "Trust me. You'll forget about her soon enough."

I hoped she was right. I never hoped for something so much in my life.

***

I sat at our usual table with two muffins placed on saucers. Two cups of steaming coffee were placed next to the plates, and I glanced at my watch every few minutes as I waited.

Taylor emerged from the crowd and headed my way. She wore skin-tight jeans with heeled boots and a brown jacket over a pink scarf. Her hair was done in curls, something she rarely did.

I was supposed to be indifferent to her.

159

But I thought she looked more beautiful than she ever had before.

"Hey." She dropped into the seat across from me and pulled her hair over one shoulder.

We hadn't spoken all week, and I only reached out to her because I was worried about her. And...I really missed her. Spending time with Julia didn't seem to make a difference. My heart belonged to this woman across from me, and there was nothing I could do to shake it.

It sucked.

"Hey."

She immediately broke off a piece of her muffin. "Thanks for the treat."

"Sure thing." I sipped my coffee just so I had something to do. "How was work?" It was the dreaded question, but I had to ask.

"It's..." She sighed and didn't finish the sentence. "Blah."

"Blah? I'm not sure that's a word."

"Actually, it is," she said. "And it perfectly describes how I feel."

"I'm sure things are getting better. Just stick to the curriculum and the common core standards, and you'll be fine. I'll help you with the next exam."

"It's not that. All the staff at the school hate me now. They think I'm incompetent."

"They do not."

"Yes, they do," she argued. "Nat told me."

Why the hell would she say that to her friend? "Who cares what they think?"

"I do," she snapped. "I work with these people every day. Of course I care."

"Well, don't. You're a damn good teacher, and I would know." I wish I could fix all of this for her, but it was out of my hands. I didn't want to tell my parents that Taylor was the teacher from Bristol Academy. It would create a lot of drama when I could just wait for it to settle down on its own. No matter what, when they figured it out, it would be awkward. But we'd cross that bridge when we came to it. "Don't let their opinions sway you. Just focus on the prize, and do what you need to do."

She stopped eating her muffin and slouched in the chair. "I want to quit, Volt. I'll live off my savings if I have to. I don't care at this point."

"You aren't quitting."

"Yes, I am. I hate it there."

"Taylor, listen to me." I was giving her sound advice, and she needed to take it. "Finish out the year then apply for a job somewhere else. It's going to be damn hard to find another job when they see that you quit in the middle of your first year. Like, really hard."

"I can get a job doing something else. It's not the end of the world."

"But teaching is what you love."

"Ha." She took a big bite of her muffin. "It doesn't love me."

"Baby, don't give up." I cringed when I realized what I just blurted out, and I had to stop myself from dragging my hands down my face. I'd never had these kinds of slip-ups before, but I was throwing that word around left and right. I didn't even call the others by that name.

Taylor was too upset to care about the endearment. "It's a hostile environment, and I don't want to be there."

"You aren't quitting. That's the end of the story."

She focused on her muffin and said nothing else. Her irritation was heavy in the air around her, building up until it formed an impenetrable haze. "Julia was nice."

It was the strangest thing, talking about her. I felt guilty, like I did something unforgivable. I slept with Julia, not just once, but several times. The sex was good, but I kept thinking about Taylor, and when we were finished, I was unsatisfied. I had to break it off with her soon. It wasn't going anywhere, and I was just wasting her time. But it was depressing to think about. If I couldn't move on with Julia, then there was no hope for me. "She's great."

"You two seem happy together."

I shrugged. "She's beautiful and everything but...I don't think it's going to work out."

"Why not?" she asked in surprise.

I wished I could just tell her the truth. I would get it off my chest, and everything would be out in the open. I wouldn't have to come up with lies all the time. "We aren't compatible. She's a little too clingy for me."

"Really? She seemed pretty amazing. Even Sage was staring at her."

"Because he's a piece of shit that doesn't deserve you." My entire body snapped, and I went into aggressive mode. I didn't care about him looking at my date. I cared that he wasn't exclusively looking at his.

Taylor didn't flinch because she was used to my angry outbursts.

"A man should never have wandering eyes, Taylor. That's bullshit."

"I don't blame him," she said. "Julia is probably the most beautiful woman I've ever seen."

"Ha." I released a sarcastic laugh. "I've seen better."

Her eyebrows shot up. "What?"

"Nothing," I said quickly. I had a problem with these passive aggressive comments, and I needed to steer away from the topic. "You shouldn't be with a guy who pays attention to the other women in the room. He should only pay attention to you."

"I know," she said. "But Julia was right in front of him. Not many other places to look."

"Why are you making excuses for him?" My temper flared all over again. I was normally sensible, but when Taylor put up with losers like him, I couldn't handle it.

"Calm down. If you were in his position, you would have stared at her too. Don't act like you wouldn't."

I looked her dead in the eye and didn't blink. "If I were with you, I wouldn't even know other people were in the restaurant. I wouldn't know if it was morning or evening because I'd be too busy looking at you to notice the sun and the moon. If I were with you, I would feel blind to the world and everything in it—because you're all that I'd see."

She stared at me for several heartbeats, her eyes locked to mine and unblinking. A strand of hair fluttered in the breeze, but she didn't tuck it behind her ear like she usually did.

I successfully made the conversation awkward, just like I always did. It was so frustrating to want a woman I could never have. I'd never been this challenged before. Not to sound like a dick, but there was never a woman I couldn't have. And now the one woman I couldn't live without didn't even notice me. I couldn't even move on with someone else because I was neck-deep in this shit.

Taylor didn't say anything, either because she was irritated with me or just uncomfortable. Maybe she was catching on to my feelings. She'd be totally ignorant to not figure it out by now. I didn't sleep with her because I had nothing else to do. I didn't hate her boyfriends because I was just protective. I didn't spend all my time with her because I didn't have any other friends.

When the silence stretched for another minute, I knew I needed to break it. "Sorry. I just can't stand cheaters. Drew was an ass, and now Sage can't keep his eyes to himself. Bothers me."

"It's one thing to look and another thing to touch."

But I wouldn't look or touch if I were with her. "What are you doing this weekend?" I didn't care about her answer, but I had to change the subject. It was growing more uncomfortable by the second.

"I don't have a lot of plans, but on Friday, I'm meeting some of Sage's friends. It's his birthday, so we're going out to dinner."

So things were getting serious. Had she slept with him? I cursed myself for even wondering about it. It didn't matter, and I would never ask because I couldn't handle the answer. "What did you get him?"

"Nothing yet. Trying to figure that out."

I had a few ideas, but they all involved sex. And I didn't want her touching him. "Maybe you could make something."

"I'm not that crafty."

"You make stuff for your classroom all the time."

"Yeah, but that's usually related to science. I don't think Sage really cares about academics."

"You'll figure it out. Can't go wrong with sports tickets."

"Hmm…that's not a bad idea." A thoughtful look came over her face. "He loves the Yankees. I'm sure he would love to go to a game."

Now I hated myself for giving her a good idea. "There you go."

She pulled out her phone and started searching for tickets. "Let's see… There's a game this Sunday. Perfect."

At least she wasn't getting him a blowjob.

"Thanks for the suggestion."

I stopped myself from gritting my teeth. "No problem."

"What are you doing this weekend?"

A whole lot of nothing. "No plans."

"Want to do something on Saturday?"

Damn. I shouldn't have said that. "Maybe." I couldn't keep spending time with her when it was just sucking me in further. Should I move away? Was that the only answer at this point? My company was expanding, so maybe I could expand with it.

"Maybe?" she asked with a laugh.

"I might have plans with Julia. Can't remember."

"I thought you were breaking up with her."

"I said I was thinking about it."

"I think you should give it another chance. Women like that don't come around very often."

Women like you don't come around very often. "I'll see where it goes."

She finished her muffin then grabbed her coffee. "Well, I should head home. I need to clean up and head to the dry cleaners."

I was sad she was leaving but also relieved. Distance was the most essential thing for me. Whenever I was with her, I was comfortable. There was nothing else in the world besides the two of us. It felt the same as sitting in front of a warm fire. I never wanted to leave. "I have stuff to take care of too." I stood up and tossed my trash. "Have fun at the birthday party."

"Thanks." She pulled her bag over her shoulder and gave me an award-winning smile. It was the kind that lit up everything near her. She was a spotlight that illuminated the entire city. After a quick wave, she walked off, her hips swaying in her skin-tight jeans. I wasn't the only one who gawked at her as she passed. Everyone on the street turned their heads in her direction.

And the entire world did too.

***

"What brings you here?" I looked up to see Derek standing over the desk.

"Just thought I would stop by on my way home."

That was unlike him unless he wanted something. "What's up?"

"How are things with Tayz going?"

"Terrible." I leaned back in the office chair and crossed my arms over my chest.

"What?" he blurted. "Julia said you guys have really hit it off."

"Ugh." I dragged my hands down my face. "She really said that?"

"Yeah. Are you telling me you've been dating that fox and still aren't over Taylor?"

It was embarrassing to admit it out loud. "I don't know what's wrong with me."

"What the hell, man?"

"I'm gonna break it off with Julia."

"What?" he shrieked. "Are you crazy?"

"Yes." I'm out of my mind. *Shit, I'm insane.* "I've tried falling for her, but nothing has changed. Taylor is still in my goddamn head all the time."

"Have you slept with Julia?"

It was none of his business, but I nodded anyway.

"And still nothing?" he asked incredulously.

"I'm telling you, I'm doomed."

"No, I think you're gay."

I grabbed the stapler and prepared to throw it at him.

"Whoa, whoa." He held up both hands. "Let's just calm down."

"I'm anything but calm right now." I set the stapler on the table with a loud thud. "I'm screwed. I'm in too deep, and I'll never get out."

"Maybe you should just tell her how you feel."

"And what's that gonna do? Make things worse?" I snapped.

"She'll reject you, and you can move on."

I couldn't handle hearing that. Even now, I still had a little hope we could be something more. When we lay together in bed, she always wrapped her arms around me. When she was upset, she'd grip my hand like she needed

170

my touch to go on. If I told her how I felt and she turned me down, that would shatter the tiny amount of hope I still possessed. And without that belief, there would be nothing holding me together. I'd rather hold on to this small amount of goodness than risk losing it altogether. "I don't want her to reject me."

"Well, if she does, you'll know it's time to move on."

"But I'll lose her friendship."

"Are you really friends now?" he challenged.

It was true that my feelings had changed the dynamic of our relationship. "If I tell her now, it'll just blow up in my face. If she were single, I could do something about it."

He rolled his eyes. "She's not engaged to the guy. Go for it."

"She's meeting his friends tomorrow. She clearly likes him."

"Whatever. All is fair in love and war."

"It's not gonna happen." I'd made my final decision.

"Then maybe you should move."

That wasn't a bad idea, but I didn't want to leave New York. I loved it there. "I was born and raised here. I don't think I could handle any other city."

"Boston is pretty close."

"No." There was nothing for me there.

Derek leaned against the desk and gave me a sympathetic look. "Then maybe you should keep dating Julia."

"No." That wasn't fair to her, even though she knew how I felt about Taylor.

"Then you're hopeless," Derek said. "I'm officially out of ideas."

I've been out of ideas for a while.

The elevator doors opened, and Clay stepped onto the floor.

That was my cue. "I've got to go, Derek. I have a client."

"I thought you didn't do the tutoring thing anymore?" he questioned.

"I have a special circumstance." I rose out of the chair and shoved my phone into my pocket. "I'll see you later."

"Alright. Until next time." Derek banged his hand on the desk before he walked into the elevator and disappeared.

I grabbed my supplies and Clay's lunch before I walked inside the tutoring room. Clay was already sitting at the desk wearing a baggy hoodie and old jeans. His hair was combed in an odd way, pushed forward and over one side of his face.

"Woke up on the wrong side of the bed?" I teased.

He immediately patted his hair down. "Need a haircut."

I set my stuff down then pushed the sandwich toward him. "I'll give you some cash."

"I'm okay." Even then, he hated taking money from me.

"If you don't get a haircut soon, you'll have to rock the ponytail look."

"I'm not a girl," he argued.

"Then let's get that haircut." I set everything up then pushed the book toward him. "Alright, we're going to start the math section. Math is about logic rather than pure mathematics. Even without a calculator, you can figure things out pretty easily based on laws and formulas. I'll show you what I mean."

He propped his chin on his hand and looked bored, only one eye visible.

His hair was distracting me because I couldn't see his entire face. He wasn't eating either, which was unlike him. Usually, he scarfed down all his food the second he walked in the door.

"Everything alright?" I asked.

"I'm fine," he answered. "Just bored."

"You won't be bored in a second." I explained the math section before I turned the workbook toward him. "Let's start with the first question. I'll work it out with you."

He grabbed the mechanical pencil and stared at the question. His eyes moved over the words several times as he tried to figure it out. Several minutes went by, and he didn't make a mark with his pencil. It took him a long time to approach the reading section of the exam, so I knew this would be even more difficult. Absentmindedly, he moved his hand over his hair and pulled it slightly to the side.

And that's when I noticed it.

He had a dark black eye, bruised and swollen. The skin surrounding it was just as damaged with popped blood vessels and discoloration. It wasn't the kind of injury you got from falling. It was the kind of bruise you got when you were punched in the face—several times.

I never knew I could be this angry. I never understood what rage really felt like until that moment. My hands shook as my lungs locked up. I couldn't breathe. I wanted to demolish the office because I didn't know how else to channel my anger. My body and mind only knew destruction.

I wanted to murder someone.

"Clay."

He flinched at the hostility in my voice. I never yelled, but my violent tone was enough to make him jerk. His eyes met mine, and when he saw the look on my face, he knew I figured it out.

"Who did this to you?" I couldn't stop shaking. All I knew was bloodlust. Someone was about to be put into the ground—six feet under.

He pulled his hair further over his face, hiding the mark. "I fell on the handle of my bike...hit me right in the eye."

"Don't. Lie. To. Me." I slid everything off the table and slammed my fists hard onto the wood. The sound echoed in the room, thudding indefinitely.

Clay immediately sat back, showing fear for the very first time.

"I'm going to ask you again, and you're going to give me the right answer."

He stared at the ground.

"It was your father, wasn't it?" I should have known when I spotted that other bruise. Clay lied to me about it, and I should have figured it out. What kind of mentor was I for not noticing sooner?

His voice came out weak. "No."

I flipped the table over and it crashed into the wall. Thankfully, no one else was there otherwise people would assume I was smacking the kid around myself. "Why do you keep lying to me?"

He stayed in the chair but leaned back as far as he could.

"I'm calling the cops." I was putting this guy behind bars for the rest of his life.

"Wait." He held up his hand, so I wouldn't walk around him. "Don't."

"Why the hell not?" My nostrils flared because I was breathing so hard.

"I don't want to go into a foster home. Please." It was the first time he ever begged for anything. "That's even worse than where I am now."

"No, it's not," I said with gritted teeth. "No one will hurt you there."

"But I'll be stuck with a bunch of other kids, I'll never be adopted, and I won't be able to leave and do what I want. I'll be a prisoner there, and they'll scrutinize my every move."

"Clay, you don't know anything about foster care."

"Yes, I do," he snapped. "I've had friends in the system, and they say it's terrible. I've only got a year and a half left, and then I can leave. I'm never home as it is, and it doesn't happen all the time. Just...don't call the cops."

"Clay, it shouldn't happen at all."

"It's really not that bad."

This kid was an enabler, and he didn't even realize it. "It's never okay to hit someone. So don't say it's not that bad. It's completely unacceptable."

"I'm not saying it's okay," he whispered. "But I can handle it."

Now I wanted to snap again. "You shouldn't have to handle it."

"Just don't call the cops. Volt, I'm begging you."

How could I sleep at night if I didn't know whether or not this kid was okay? Over the past few months, I'd grown fonder of him than I had of any other student in the past. I cared about him. No, I loved him. "I'm sorry. I can't let you keep living there."

"No." He jumped to his feet and faced me. "Stay out of it, alright? I'm telling you I don't want to go into foster care. I'd rather keep everything the same. I'm careful around my dad, but sometimes, he drinks too much and things happen. It's not like it happens all the time."

I hated listening to him justify his father's actions. It was sickening.

"If you call the cops, I'll deny everything."

"That bruise will speak for itself."

"Volt, you don't get it because you come from a different world with a mom and a dad who love you. You don't know what it's like to struggle. You don't know what it's like to survive. You don't understand how the real system works. You think sending me to child protective services is going to help me but it's not. It's just going to make my life more difficult. I don't have much time left. I'm almost out of there. Please don't ruin this for me."

My body couldn't digest all the pain and rage. Instead of subsiding, it just bubbled and became worse. I felt the agony intensify into something blinding. I'd never understood the kind of pain Clay had been through, but just the mere idea of it killed me inside.

"Volt, please." He blocked my way to the door. "I know this is hard, but please let it go."

"How can I do nothing?" I whispered. "He might kill you."

"He won't. He just gets angry and pushes me around. But he's never taken it that far."

"Yet," I said bitterly.

"Promise me you won't tell anyone."

How could I ever make that kind of promise?

"Volt, come on. You're the only person I have in my life right now. You're the only person I can trust. Please, help me."

"Letting you live there isn't helping you."

"And dragging me out is worse," he argued. "Volt, please. I'm begging you."

I put my hands on my hips and tried to sort this out. I was at a crossroads, and I didn't know what to do. This kid deserved better than the treatment he was getting, but I didn't know what the solution was. He was adamant about avoiding foster care, and I understood why. But could I let him stay with an abuser? It was only for another year and a half, but was that too long? "Clay, I'm sorry. I have to tell someone."

All hope left his face, and rage quickly replaced it. "I thought you were my friend..."

"I am your friend."

"Friends don't do that to each other. I'm telling you what I want, but you won't give it to me."

"I'm trying to look after you."

"Well, don't," he snapped. "If you put me in a foster home, I'm just going to run away."

"Clay, someone could adopt you."

"Are you kidding me?" he yelled. "No one is going to adopt a sixteen-year-old misfit. Let's not play fairytale, all right? I'm going to sleep in a room with thirty other kids, with a curfew and shit, and those kids are going to be worse than my dad. At least where I'm at now, I have the freedom to do things. If I'm locked up, I'll be a prisoner. Don't rat me out. If I'd known you would do this, I never would have come here. I trusted you, and now I feel stupid."

My heart ached in the most painful way. "Clay, you can trust me."

"No, I can't. I'm asking you to help me and you won't."

"I am helping you."

"Then let it go. I'd gladly take a bruise once in a while over ending up in a place like that." He stayed in front of the door, but the fight was no longer in him. He stared at me with contempt, like he hated me more than the man who abused him.

And that hurt.

There was no right answer, and everything was in shades of gray. But the way Clay glared at me with hatred was the most difficult of all. It didn't matter if he liked me, but I wanted him to trust me. And if I did this, I suspected our relationship would be over.

Clay looked away, unable to stare at me anymore.

Unsure what else to do, I gave in. "Okay."

He looked back at me, one of his eyebrows raised.

"I won't say anything. But are you sure this is what you want?"

"Yes." He said it without hesitation. "I'm never home anyway. These fights only happen once in a while. In sixteen months, I'll be out of the house and living somewhere else. I've dealt with it my whole life. I can deal with it a little longer."

How would I be able to sleep at night not knowing if he was okay? How would I be able to forgive myself if something happened to him? "I'm here if you need anything. If things get bad, just leave and call me. I'll come get you wherever you are. I'm here—always."

"I know, Volt." Now that he got his way, he relaxed and gave me that same look I was used to. The fondness returned, and he was at ease. "I appreciate you caring about me. Really. Most people don't."

"That's not true."

"It is," he said. "And that's okay since I have at least one person who does."

***

I had an address and a face.

I knew exactly what I was looking for.

It was three in the morning when I made my move. He headed down the street in a dark blue hoodie with his hands in his pockets. He was unnaturally thin, reminding me of Clay in more ways than he should.

He turned the corner and walked down a dark alleyway between a Chinese restaurant and a laundromat. A man was sitting there in a dark leather jacket. Both of his hands were in his pockets, and he didn't look my way.

Silently, Clay's father pulled out the cash and handed it over. In exchange, he got a small plastic bag wrapped up tightly. He shoved it into his pocket so quickly I couldn't see what it was.

The dealer turned the opposite direction and walked up the alleyway, counting the cash that he'd just received.

When Clay's father turned around, he didn't look at me, dismissing me for another outcast. His hands were shoved firmly into his pockets, and his hood was pulled over his head.

Just looking at him made me sick. I hated this man even though we'd never met, and killing him was all I could think about. I wanted to wrap my hands around his throat and choke him until he couldn't breathe. I wanted to break both of his arms so he could never lay a hand on Clay again.

I wanted to do so much worse.

Just before he left the alleyway, I made my move.

I snatched him by the back of the sweater and yanked him to the ground, forcing him to his back on the slick concrete. A streetlight was forty feet away, but the Chinese restaurant blocked most of the light. Visibility was poor, and he would never get a good look at my face.

"What the fuck, asshole?" He rolled to his feet quickly. "Get your own."

I snatched him again then threw him against the wall. The air left his lungs once he smacked into the concrete. His arms were twigs, and his lack of muscle made him pathetically weak. When he tried to push me off, it felt like a child pushing me.

I slugged him hard in the face, hitting him right in the eye. I got so much gratification from scarring him the way he scarred Clay. This man needed to suffer forever. I would never let him forget this night. I would never let him think he could touch Clay again.

I wailed on him, slamming my fist into his face and then his stomach. I bruised most of his skin, making him weak from the pain and loss of blood. I beat him to within mere inches of his life, making him sway like he was boneless.

I dropped him to the ground and leaned over him, my hood covering my face. Even if he knew what I looked like, he would have no way of finding me. But it was better to be safe than sorry.

His face was bloody and his eyes were swollen shut. Blood dripped from the corner of his mouth and rolled down his cheek. When he coughed, disgusting shit came up.

"Listen to me." I grabbed him by the throat and squeezed. "Touch Clay again and this will end quite differently."

He groaned then released a painful cough.

"Do you understand me?"

"Yes...yes."

I squeezed him tighter. "Touch a single hair on his head, and I'll end you. You got it?"

His breathing grew deep and raspy. "Who are you?"

I punched him in the face harder than ever.

"Fuck." He tried to grab his nose, but I stepped on his hand.

"If you hurt him, I'll know about it. You threaten him, I'll know about it. Do anything to that kid, utter a single word about this, and I'll hunt you down again and do something far worse."

He fought to breathe but my hold on him was too tight. He gasped for air that he couldn't reach.

"Do we have an understanding?" I wasn't leaving until I had confirmation that Clay wouldn't pay for this. That he would be untouched after my actions.

"Yes," he gasped.

I squeezed him harder, choking him out. "Are you sure?"

Now he could hardly speak. He moved his mouth but nothing came out. "Yes..."

I finally released my hold on his throat. He was beaten bloody, and those bruises and cuts would take weeks to heal. Every time he looked in the mirror, he would have a reminder of what happened tonight.

And he wouldn't even think of touching Clay.

Chapter Ten

Taylor

I was meeting Sage and his friends for a birthday dinner, and I was a little nervous about the evening. There would be a lot of new people I'd never met, and I'd probably be interrogated the whole time.

But Volt interrogated all my men, so this was fair.

I walked down the street with his gift tucked under my arm. It was the baseball tickets wrapped in navy blue wrapping paper. I made him a special card by hand, decorating it to make the gift more personal.

I was just around the corner when my phone started to ring.

Volt was calling me.

Now wasn't the best time for a chat, but I couldn't ignore his call. It went against everything my body wanted, so I swiped the call button before I held it to my ear. "Heeey. Whatcha doing?" We hadn't spoken in nearly a week, and it always felt strange when we had periods of silence.

He was silent.

"Volt?" I thought I could hear him breathing.

He still didn't say anything.

I stopped walking altogether even though I was right in front of the restaurant. "Volt, are you there?"

When his voice came through the line, it sounded broken—beyond repair. "Hey."

I knew there was something seriously wrong. Not just a little wrong—but extremely. Volt had hit rock bottom. But how he got there was a mystery. "What is it? Are you okay?"

"I need you to come to my apartment."

He never commanded me to do things. He usually asked. "I can be there in ten minutes."

"Thank you." He hung up immediately, like staying on the line for a second more was too much for him to handle.

I heard the line go dead, and I slowly lowered the phone. My heart was beating hard, and I felt sick to my stomach. Something was wrong with Volt, and I was pretty sure his heart was broken.

"Hey." Sage approached from the entryway of the restaurant. "Perfect timing. I already have a glass of wine for you."

I forgot about Sage's birthday altogether once I spoke to Volt. Now it seemed insignificant. "Uh..."

"Something wrong?" He spotted the shocked look on my face. "What is it?"

"I'm so sorry, Sage. But I have to go."

"You have to go?" he asked. "But you're already here."

"I know, I'm so sorry. But I have to go to Volt. I'll try to come back as soon as I can."

His face contorted from disappointment to anger. "Volt? Why do you have to go to him?"

I didn't want to give my answer. "I'm not sure. But there's something wrong."

"Well...all of my friends are sitting inside waiting to see you. Not to mention, it's my birthday. You're really just going to leave? Did someone die?"

"I don't know yet. He didn't say."

"Can it wait?"

Volt wouldn't have called me unless it was important. "I'll make it up to you. I swear."

"Well, my birthday doesn't come for another year, so you'll have to wait a long time."

"I feel terrible about this. I really do." I was making a terrible first impression with his friends, not to mention pissing him off. "I'm so sorry."

"Then don't do it. It's as simple as that." He challenged me with his look, warning me if I left, there would be serious consequences. Even our relationship was on the line, and it dangled on the edge of a knife.

"He needs me. He's my best friend."

"Shouldn't I be your best friend?" he challenged. "And shouldn't you be there for me?"

"Sage, I know you're upset, but whatever Volt is going through must be serious. He wouldn't have called me otherwise. He knows I'm going out for your birthday. He helped me pick out the gift."

"Don't you think that's a strange coincidence?"

"What?"

"That he called when he knows you're with me?"

I didn't understand his meaning until it dawned on me. "You really think he's still into me? How much clearer do I have to make it? Volt doesn't see me like that. You saw his girlfriend."

"But he still calls you for everything. Why isn't he calling her?"

"I...I don't know." If something were seriously wrong, I would want him to call me and no one else. And that realization made me feel a little faint.

"Whatever." He threw his arms up. "Go to him. Have fun."

"Sage, someone could be dead." *How could he be so selfish?*

"If someone were dead, he would have told you."

"You don't know that." I'm the only one who knew him well enough to make such a claim.

"I've always thought he had a thing for you, but you know what? Now I think you have a thing for him." He gave me a mirthless glare, the kind that showed the depth of his anger. People passed us on the sidewalk, but he didn't glance at them and neither did I.

"That's not true."

"It's not?" He tilted his head to the side, looking maniacal. "Because it sure seems like it."

"Volt has been a good friend to me since I moved here. I didn't know anyone in the city, and he helped me. He helped me with work, and he's always looked after me. Maybe you don't understand what friendship is like, but I do. Stop overanalyzing everything. You're seeing things that aren't there."

"Oh, really?" he asked. "I'll tell you what I see, Taylor. It's my birthday, and you're choosing to be with him. Plain and simple."

I was wasting time in this argument. Volt needed me and five minutes had already passed. I had no idea what happened to him, but not knowing was crippling. "I'm not choosing to be with him. Something has happened to him, and I need to be there. I'm sorry it's on the night of your birthday, but friends are always there for each other no matter what. If anything, you should be understanding. You're making this entirely about yourself."

"I should be understanding?" he asked incredulously. "He didn't even tell you what's wrong. And you're running off to him."

"He'll tell me when I get there."

"That's still strange. If his mother passed away, then fine. For all we know, you're going to get there and he's going to ask you to help him pick an outfit. And you'll run off for no reason."

"First of all, he would never call me for something like that." I held up my hand to him, growing angry at his comments. "Second of all, being a good friend isn't about asking questions. It's about being there for someone else.

192

I'm sorry that I've ruined your birthday, and your friends will probably never like me now, but Volt is family."

"He's family?" he snapped.

That wasn't the smartest thing to say, but the damage was done. "Yes. He's family."

"Fine. You've made it clear he's more important than I am." He stepped back, his arms still in the air. "Have a good night."

"Sage, I never said that."

"You don't need to say it." He turned his back to me and walked away. "You've made it pretty clear."

***

I burst into his apartment and found him sitting on the couch. A glass of scotch sat next to a nearly empty bottle. Volt reclined against the cushion, his head tilted back and his face toward the ceiling.

This was bad.

I set Sage's gift on the counter then moved to his side. He smelled like scotch, masking his cologne and natural scent. The booze burned as it entered my nostrils. "Volt, what's wrong?" I scooted close to him and wrapped my arm around his.

He stared at the ceiling for another minute before he sat up and looked at me. The depression in his eyes told a story more painful than anything I'd ever encountered. Without saying a word, he told me about his heartbreak.

When I looked down, I noticed his hands. They were swollen and bruised, caked with dried blood and missing pieces of flesh. His knuckles were hard to distinguish because they were massacred. "Volt..." I grabbed one hand and examined it, seeing the extent of the damage.

"Clay." That was all he said. He stared at his hands without reacting. Whatever pain he felt was numbed. Or perhaps he was just used to feeling it. "Clay came into my office yesterday with a black eye. His father did it."

I wrapped my hand around his wrist because I couldn't touch his hand. It was too broken for a simple caress. Without hearing the entire story, I knew exactly what happened. Volt flipped a switch and attacked Clay's father. Not once did I judge him for it. "I'm so sorry."

"I hunted him down when he was buying weed and made him pay for what he did. I beat him to within an inch of his life. Not once did I feel bad about it. I still don't feel bad about it."

I ran my hand up and down his arm, soothing him the only way I knew how. "Did you call the police?"

"No." His voice broke. "Clay asked me not to."

"Why not?"

"He doesn't want to go to a foster home. He begged me not to say anything. So, I gave him what he wanted. But I had to make sure his father never lays a hand on him again. I'm pretty sure I scared the shit out of that bastard."

My hand stopped at his forearm. "Volt, you have to tell the police. You can't let Clay keep living there."

"I don't want him there either," he whispered. "But he fought me on it—hard. He said he would never forgive me if I went through with it."

"That shouldn't matter, Volt. You need to do the best thing for him."

He looked away, his lips pressed tightly together. "I'm all the kid has. I'm the only person he trusts. And if he turns away from me...who will he have then?"

Volt had a great relationship with this boy, and I understood why he wanted to keep that friendship. But he had to do the right thing—no matter the cost. "He'll be mad at you for a while. But one day, he'll thank you."

195

"No, he won't," he whispered. "I handled the situation the best way I could. His father would be stupid to do anything to Clay. Next time, I'll really kill him."

"Unless he kills Clay first."

His skin immediately turned ice-cold. "The thought scares me."

"You have to go to the police, Volt."

"Clay said he would deny everything. And he would run away. The kid doesn't want to go, Taylor. I can't make him."

I was pressing an argument Volt didn't want to listen to. He was shaken up over what happened, and I wasn't helping the situation. He needed comfort and support, not a battle.

"I feel like a monster…"

I watched his face and saw the dullness enter his eyes. I'd never seen him look so low, seen him fall so hard. "That's not true."

"I beat the shit out of that loser you dated, and then I nearly killed Clay's father. I'm just so angry… I get angry when bad things happen to good people. Clay deserves more than the shit he's been given. You deserve a man who

196

would die for you. The world is so fucked up that I don't understand it."

I ran my hand up and down his arm, smelling the liquor in the air. "Clay will be okay, Volt."

"He just wants a better life for himself. But all this shit keeps holding him back." He shook his head. "How is that fair? I grew up in a perfect home with perfect parents. And he struggles just to survive another day. I don't get it." He ran his fingers through his hair then cringed when pain shot up his arm. He lowered it again, resting it on the couch.

"He'll get through it, Volt."

A distant look came into his eyes, and I knew he slipped away.

I stared at his hands again and knew if I didn't attend to them, he never would. I grabbed some supplies from his bathroom then cleaned up his hands. They were cracked and still slightly bleeding. I rubbed Neosporin into all the cuts and patted them dry before I wrapped his knuckles in gauze. I'd never done anything like this before but the technique came to me naturally.

Volt sat there, silent and still as a statue.

I clipped the gauze in place and set everything on the table before I handed him two painkillers.

He eyed them then pushed them away. Maybe it was because he drank too much or because he wanted to feel the pain. I would never know.

I moved in close to him and ran my fingers through his hair, comforting him with my touch. The smell of booze was overwhelming so I breathed through my mouth to avoid it. Even then, it burned my throat on the way down.

Volt turned his face toward me and watched me caress him. The distant look was still in his eyes, that drunken stupor I had never seen before. His reactions were slow and drawn out. His breathing was deeper than usual, and sometimes his eyes drooped like he might fall asleep.

I fingered his thick dark hair and felt the softness slide through my fingertips. His hair was slightly curly at the ends when he let it grow out enough. I'd never really explored him like this before. We'd hugged, even kissed, but I'd never comforted him quite like this.

His hand moved to my thigh and he squeezed it gently despite the pain it must've caused his knuckles. His fingers covered my entire thigh because his hand was so big. He could break my leg with a single movement if he wanted to.

Silently, he moved his gaze to mine and looked me in the eyes. He stared at me without blinking, searching for something only he could find. Our faces were just inches apart, and every breath reeked of the scotch he drank. He wasn't himself, and I could feel the change in the air, the tingle that accompanied a special moment.

His eyes glanced at my lips.

I could feel the stare burn my mouth. I could feel his want and his desire. It burned me like the white-hot sun. But it was the kind of burn that felt good. The kind that made you feel warm in the midst of winter.

The alcohol was guiding him forward, and he lost his inhibitions quickly. Before he made the move, I knew it was coming. I could feel it in the air. The intensity shivered my spine.

He moved closer to me, his face slowly approaching mine. His eyes were still on my lips, studying them like a work of art.

My heart wouldn't slow down.

His hand left my thigh and moved up my body until it reached my neck. Once his hand touched me, warm and calloused, I felt my breath hitch. His fingers dug into the bottom of my hair, touching me in a way he never did before.

I couldn't breathe.

I remained still even though I knew exactly what would happen next. He was drunk out of his mind and not thinking clearly. His choices were made in a place other than his brain.

But I didn't move away.

His hand moved to my cheek, his fingertips feeling the softness. He studied my face as he touched me, memorizing my features. His eyes were no longer hooded. They gazed at me without blinking, not wanting to miss a single moment.

His thumb drifted to my mouth and rested in the corner. He brushed the tip along my bottom lip, feeling every groove of my mouth. He leaned into me, getting closer than he ever had before.

His intensity was enough to burn me. I could feel it in every corner of the room. I could feel the pleasure before we even touched. I could feel the electricity without the plug.

He pressed his face against mine, his lips just inches away. His breath washed over me, and I could hear his excitement with every exhalation. His thumb brushed along my lip before it returned to my cheek.

And then he kissed me.

He pressed his soft lips against mine, his face tilted slightly to the right. Instead of feeling awkward or strange, I felt heat rush up my spine and directly into my brain. My body lit on fire, and I couldn't think straight. All I felt was blinding pleasure, the kind that radiated to every cell of my body.

And that was just the first second.

He moved his mouth against mine, brushing our lips past one another. They danced to a song that wasn't playing, and they fell into a natural rhythm.

My hand dug into his hair, and I gripped the strands as he continued to kiss me. It wasn't the kind of kiss I expected him to have with anyone. It was slow and agonizing, just as much of a tease as it was satisfying.

Volt wrapped his other arm around my waist and pulled me closer to him, our chests touching as our mouths continued to move together. His desperation was obvious in every caress. He didn't just want this kiss but needed it.

And I think I needed it too.

He parted my mouth just enough to give me his tongue, and that was even better than his lips. He breathed into me at the same time, making me come alive with every embrace.

My body melted and became boneless. All I could feel was a shock running through my veins. It felt so good, just like the last time we kissed. I was so high on depression that I wondered if it was really that good.

But it was.

Volt pulled me onto his lap, so I was straddling his hips and feeling his hard-on through his jeans. He deepened the kiss and pulled me further into him, wanting as much as he could have.

And that's when I realized this needed to stop.

He was drunk and out of his mind, probably ten times above the legal driving limit, and he wasn't thinking clearly. He was just doing whatever was necessary to make himself feel better.

I couldn't let it go on.

I found the strength to pull away and end the hottest kiss I'd ever had. I looked into his eyes and saw that same look of desire. He didn't want it to end either. To him, it had only just begun.

I moved off his lap, putting necessary distance between us. "Let's get you into bed."

He remained seated, still staring at me. His lips were slightly parted like my mouth should still be glued to his.

Redness burned in my cheeks so I busied myself cleaning up his mess of booze. Sage and I just broke up, so I didn't need to feel guilty for kissing Volt, but it was still a low thing to do. Volt was drunk and had no idea what he was doing. He probably wouldn't even remember it the next morning. I took advantage of him when I shouldn't have.

And he would never do that to me.

***

I was wrapped up in Volt's arms when we woke up the next morning. It was twelve thirty in the afternoon and far later than it should've been. His chest was pressed to my back, and with every breath he took, I felt it rise against me.

He stirred and released a quiet moan. "Fuck, my head hurts."

I grabbed the two pills from the nightstand and a glass of water. "Here you go."

He rubbed the sleep from his eyes before he swallowed the pills and downed the water. His hair was a mess from my fingers constantly running through it, and his hands were still bandaged. He took a look around the room before his eyes settled on me.

Judging the look on his face, he didn't remember anything from the night before. He probably wasn't even sure how I got there or why I was in this bed with him. It took him a few minutes to come back to the moment. "I'm not sure what happened. I remembered drinking. And I think I remember you coming over. But I don't remember much else."

So he didn't remember.

Phew.

"You told me what happened with Clay, and we sat together on the couch for a while."

He nodded slowly. "Nightmare from hell."

"I bandaged up your hands because they looked terrible."

"Thanks…" He examined each one. "I hope they look better than they feel."

"I doubt it."

He ran his fingers through his hair before he lay back again, shirtless. "It's one of those days when I don't want to get up."

"You don't have to. I'll make you some breakfast."

"You don't need to make me anything."

"I don't mind. You cook for me all the time."

"But that's different," he said. "You're my lady." He fumbled for the right words. "I mean, you're *a* lady."

"I don't mind whipping up something." I jumped out of bed wearing his shorts and t-shirt. Everything was too big and baggy, but at least it was comfortable. I walked into the kitchen and found a box of pancake mix and some eggs.

Volt walked out ten minutes later, his perfect chest highlighted with muscle and strength. His stomach was lined with abs, and his arms were carved with muscle. I knew he had a nice body, but when he displayed it like that, it made me uncomfortable.

Because he was hot.

I thought about that kiss again. The way his mouth felt against mine was unreal. It burned me in so many good ways, lighting me on fire and making me sizzle like oil in a hot pan. It made the blood rush to my head and other places. Thankfully, he couldn't remember. Otherwise, I wouldn't be able to look him in the eye.

His sweatpants hung low on his hips, showing the noticeable V that reached up from underneath his clothes.

He poured himself a fresh cup of coffee and drank it black. "You really don't need to make me anything."

"Well, I'm almost done so it doesn't matter."

He sipped his coffee at the counter and noticed the small package I left sitting there. It was the gift for Sage. The gift I would never give him. It would be weird to go to the game with someone else, so I would just sell them on Stub Hub. "What's this?"

"Nothing," I said as I shoveled the pancakes onto a plate. "Just Sage's birthday gift."

"And why is it here?"

"I had it on me at the time."

He continued to examine it before he set it down. The realization came into his eyes, and he understood the significance. "Shit, I'm sorry. Last night was his birthday, wasn't it?"

"Yeah...but it's not a big deal." I wasn't going to make him feel bad for needing me. And I wasn't going to make him feel like shit for being the reason I got dumped.

"I totally forgot. Taylor, I'm sorry." He set his cup down and gave me a sad look. He didn't need to tell me he was sorry because I could see it written all over his face.

"It's really okay. Don't even worry about it."

"I'm sure he was pissed."

"He wasn't. We just rescheduled for another day."

He finally relaxed when he realized he didn't ruin anything. "Well, I'm still sorry. I was drunk out of my mind and wasn't thinking clearly."

I knew that all too well. "I know." I set the plate on the table along with the maple syrup. "Now eat something. You'll feel better."

He sat down and helped himself to the piles of food. "Thanks. You're a good wife."

The idea of being married to him, having sex with him every day, and sleeping with him every night gave me a serious bout of chills. They ran up and down my body, making me come alive. I almost dropped my coffee because it shook me up so badly. The fact that picture looked so appealing freaked me out the most. "Wife Sife…" That barely rhymed and it didn't make sense, but it was all I could think of.

Volt didn't tease me for it. "Did I do anything stupid last night?"

Other than kissing me until my lips quivered, nothing. "No. You were pretty quiet."

"That's good. I'm glad I didn't chase you away."

Just the opposite. "You were fine. Just sad."

"Well, that makes sense because I've never been so miserable." He kept eating, but his eyes were glued to his plate.

"Clay will be okay."

"I know," he said. "But he shouldn't have to go through that at all. Any man who hits a child is a sick motherfucker."

I didn't flinch at his profanity since it was appropriate—in this instance.

"I'm sure his father won't touch him again. It would be stupid to do so."

"Yeah, he probably won't. But for how long?" Despite what Clay wanted, I didn't think he should stay in that house. He should go into protective custody, and then a foster home. No child should be afraid in his own house.

"At least a year and a half."

"But the father is getting away with a crime." I shouldn't argue about this now, but the whole situation bothered me.

"It's what Clay wants. I tried to argue with him but he refused."

"He's a child. He doesn't know anything."

"He knows more than you think," he said defensively. "Kids like him get by because they have to survive every day. Maybe he's not skilled in math and English, but he's a smart kid. He knows how the real world works. He knows how to solve complex problems. Give him more credit than that."

"I didn't mean to insult him," I said calmly. "But I think, as adults, we should take care of him."

"And I did," he said darkly. "I almost killed a man. I made him shit his pants because he was so scared. A coward like that will do anything to avoid getting his face crushed in."

Volt was getting worked up again, so I backed off. "How's your food?"

"Delicious. Thank you." He gave me a playful tap under the table.

When he touched me, I felt the excitement all over again.

What the hell was wrong with me?

"Are you seeing Sage today?"

I probably wouldn't see him ever again. "No. I'm free."

"You wanna go to the movies then?"

"You don't have plans with Julia?" He told me he was going to stop seeing her, and I was curious to know if that happened yet.

"No." He drank his coffee.

"Are you still seeing her?"

"Technically. I haven't had a chance to break it off with her yet."

I wondered if they were exclusive. Because if they were, he cheated on her last night—with me. And that made me feel like a slut.

"Why?"

I shrugged. "Just curious."

***

After the movies and dinner, we headed back to his place. I wanted to spend the night again because I didn't want to walk home.

And I wanted to be with him.

I should have run after Sage and tried to make up for what I did, but there was no motivation. When I told him Volt needed me, he kept making everything about himself and his birthday. I admit it was a dick move on my part, but he should have been more understanding and less childish. And I didn't want to leave Volt because I knew he was still down. If he drank that much to begin with, he was spiraling out of control.

Volt must have assumed I was spending the night because he handed me some clothes before he sat on the couch. "What do you want to watch?"

"I don't care." I sat beside him and pulled a blanket over my knees.

"There's basketball. Is that cool?"

"Sure." I purposely kept some space between us but at the same time, I wished that space wasn't there. All I could think about was that kiss. A part of me wanted to get him drunk all over again just so we could do it—without him remembering.

And I realized how creepy that made me sound.

"What are you doing for Thanksgiving?"

"Going home to see my family." I would be there for a few days. It would be nice to see my parents. I didn't see them as much as I would've liked. I talked to them even less.

"In Washington?"

"Yeah."

"Cool."

"You're having dinner with your parents?" He mentioned something before.

"I was until they changed their plans."

"What are they doing now?"

"My mom has been wanting to go on a trip for a while, and she convinced my dad to take her on a cruise of the Mediterranean. So, I don't have any plans."

"Oh really?" I asked in surprise. "Will you see your brother?"

"Nah. We aren't close."

I wondered if there was a story there, but I knew I shouldn't ask. If he wanted me to know, he would have told me. "Want to come with me to Washington?" I wasn't thinking when I asked. I just didn't want him to be alone on Thanksgiving. He already had a lot on his mind. Being lonely would just make it worse.

"Seriously? To meet your folks?"

"They're really nice. I think you'll like them."

"I'm sure I will. I just… Do you think that will give them the wrong impression?"

I'd never brought a man around before. I'd never had anyone serious enough to introduce to them. "I'll tell them we're just good friends. They won't look too much into it."

"Then I would love to." He gave me that smile that was in his eyes, not just his mouth. He seemed genuinely excited to visit my family, not just saying yes out of obligation.

"Cool. You'll like Washington. It's beautiful."

"I've heard that before. It's probably a lot different than New York."

"Completely."

He leaned back against the couch and stole some of the blanket. "Don't be a hog, alright?"

"I'm not a hog. Do you hear me going oink oink?"

"No," he said with a grin. "But I'd like to."

"Yeah right. Like I'd ever do that."

He stuck his hands in my sides and tickled me. "I'm not gonna stop until you do it."

I laughed and writhed underneath his attack, trying to get away from him. His massive size held me down, and I was unable to squirm away. "Oh my god, stop!"

"Say it." He dug his fingers into my armpits and showed no mercy.

These tickles were going to kill me. "Fine! Oink oink!"

He pulled his hands away and chuckled. "You're one cute pig, Tayz."

"Thanks for the compliment..." I sat upright and fixed my hair. It was all over the place and full of tangles.

"No problem." He nudged me in the side before he returned to watching TV.

I pulled the blanket farther over my legs because they were getting cold. His apartment was always freezing because he liked it that way. I didn't.

He eyed me when I pulled the blanket farther over him, and that threatening look was back in his eyes.

"You want to get tickled?" I threatened. "Because two can play that game."

He pulled the blanket off and prepared his hands. "Game on."

***

When I opened my front door, I expected to see Volt on the other side. He was probably stopping by on his way home, something he used to do a few months ago. We started spending more time together recently, and now I fell right back into that funk.

But it was Sage.

He stood with his hands in his pockets, his blue eyes looking slightly dangerous. He didn't seem happy to see me, but he didn't seem pissed either.

Unsure why he was there, I didn't say anything. Did he come to yell at me more? Did he leave something at my apartment? Break ups were hard enough, and they were even worse when you had to see each other after.

"Hi…"

"Hey." I crossed my arms over my chest. "Did you leave something here?" Because he could have texted me and asked me to mail it.

"No. I was hoping we could talk."

About what? "Uh, sure." I opened the door and he followed me in. "I'm sorry about what happened with Volt. I understand why you were so angry. I hope you still had a good birthday." There was no reason why we couldn't end on good terms.

"Actually, I came to apologize. You were right. I made everything about myself when I shouldn't have. Your friend needed your help, and you should have been there. I let my jealousy get to me."

He was apologizing? Now I felt like an even bigger bitch for kissing Volt. "Oh..."

"What was the problem, if you don't mind me asking?"

"Well...there's this kid that Volt tutors. He's in a bad situation at home and stuff. When he came to one of their tutoring sessions, he was banged up from being smacked around by his father. Volt was trying to figure out what to do to help him."

"Oh shit." Guilt spread across his face. "I didn't realize..."

"It's okay. You didn't know."

"Now I feel like a bigger ass."

Not as much as I did. "Did you have a good birthday?"

"Yeah. But it wasn't the same without you."

My heart softened and so did my eyes.

"I just didn't want us to be mad at each other anymore. I miss you and I feel guilty for the things I said. Can we have dinner together? Catch a movie or something?"

Now I was even more confused. "I thought we broke up..."

"No," he said quickly. "I'm sorry I made you think that. I let my temper get away from me. I guess I'll always be jealous of Volt. Even with a girlfriend, I see him still look at you in a special way. Julia doesn't get that look."

Volt didn't see me like that, but nothing I said would change Sage's mind.

"I don't want to break up," he whispered.

I couldn't just go to dinner without telling him what happened. Even if Volt didn't remember it, it still happened. It would be deceitful not to say anything. Could I carry a secret like that forever? "Sage, there's something I need to tell you..."

"What's up?" He tried to hide the unease in his eyes but it was futile. "You aren't ending things with me, right?" His voice remained calm but his body language said otherwise. "Because I think we just got off on the wrong foot."

"No, that's not it. But...I did think we were broken up."

He didn't catch my drift. He stared at me with the same confusion that never melted away.

"The other night, Volt was really drunk, and he kissed me. I kissed him back for a while, maybe a minute.

Then we stopped, and it was over. He doesn't remember anything because he was so messed up. But I do. I thought you and me were broken up, so I let it happen. I'm sorry..." I felt like the most terrible person on the planet. Drew cheated on me, and I was devastated. To be played like a fool was unbearable. The fact I did something similar to another person made me hate myself a little bit.

Sage dragged his hand across his chin as he looked into my kitchen. His scruff was coming in from not shaving that morning. His eyes weren't as vulnerable as they were just a moment ago because he was trying to hide everything he felt. "I can't pretend that doesn't bother me."

"You have every right to be mad." I wouldn't make excuses for what I did. I assumed we were broken up when I should have waited for another conversation. We left on such bad terms that I figured we would never work things out.

"Would you have kissed him if you thought otherwise?" He turned his eyes back on me, watching every move I made.

"Of course not." Even before Drew, I wasn't a cheater. And I would never be a cheater.

"I'm sorry, but I have to ask… Do you have feelings for him? Because you told me you didn't, but then you kissed him. What am I supposed to think?"

He was wrong to make jealous assumptions before, but now he had every right to ask that question. "I…I don't think so."

"*You don't think so?*" His hand was still on his chin, and his eyebrows were raised. "Because that's not a straightforward answer."

Growing flustered, I crossed my arms over my chest again. "He's always been just a friend to me. But when we kissed…I did like it." I felt bad saying these things to Sage, but I had to be honest. "I don't know if that means something, or if it's just a physical attraction. Maybe I'm reading too much into it, or maybe I'm not looking into it enough."

He stared at the floor, refusing to make eye contact with me. "I stand by what I said. He's into you."

"I don't think you're right about that." That was the one thing I was certain of.

"Really?" He looked at me again. "Then why did he kiss you?"

"Because he was drunk off his ass. He doesn't even remember it. Volt is the kind of guy who will kiss any woman he sees. I'm not special."

"You're more special than you think you are," he whispered.

I shifted my weight and felt the floorboards creak underneath me. My apartment was old, ancient.

"Maybe it was just lust," he said. "That's a natural emotion."

"Maybe…" I still didn't know.

"I'm not saying it doesn't bother me, but I understand why things happened the way they did. I behaved like a jerk the other night. Instead of throwing a tantrum, I should have been more understanding. My jealousy got the best of me. I don't care about my birthday or the fact you were going to meet my friends. I cared that you were choosing him over me."

"That's not how it was, Sage. If I were with him and you told me you needed me, I would be there. It wouldn't matter if it were his birthday or some other special occasion."

"I know," he said with a nod.

It was unclear where we stood, even with the apologies. When I kissed Volt, there was no going back. I wasn't thinking clearly at the time, just feeling our lips move together in the most natural way possible. Even when he was drunk, Volt was the best kisser I'd ever been with— and that included Sage. Volt had more experience than any other man since he'd locked lips with every woman in Manhattan, so I attributed the sparks to his batting average.

"I'd like to give this another chance."

Shocked, I stared at him with wide eyes.

"I'm not saying the kiss with Volt doesn't bother me because it does, but the whole incident was my fault. If I hadn't pushed you away, you wouldn't have let the kiss happen. And it sounds pretty innocent anyway."

It was innocent because it didn't last long. But in intensity, it was the complete opposite.

"I really like you, Taylor. Can we try this again?"

I didn't expect Sage to fight for me like this. He'd always been jealous of Volt, so I thought we were through when that kiss happened. But he was still there. "Do your friends hate me?"

He shrugged. "They aren't your biggest fan right now…but that's because of me."

"Great..."

"But I haven't met Sara yet. You can talk shit about me before I meet her. Ya know, even the score." He gave me a slight smile, the kind that made his eyes twinkle with happiness.

When he was cute like that, he was hard to resist. "I don't think I could ever talk shit about you. Not when you're so sweet."

"Well, I wasn't very sweet the other night."

"But you are now. And that's what counts."

"So...does that mean we're okay?"

"I think so."

He closed the gap between us and wrapped his arms around my waist. He pulled me hard against his chest and pressed his forehead to mine, holding me the way I liked.

"Do you have plans tonight?"

"Yes. With you."

"Well, I got you Yankees tickets for your birthday. And the game starts in an hour."

"Wow. That's a great gift."

"You wanna go?"

"Absolutely."

Chapter Eleven

Volt

I broke it off with Julia.

"I don't understand." She faced me in her living room, her arms across her boobalicious chest. She had a nice body and a beautiful face, the kind of looks that guys would kill for. "We have such great chemistry."

No. I'm just good in bed. "You're great, Julia. Really. But...I'm just not invested in this relationship."

"Is this because of Taylor?" Jealousy rang in her tone, and it was the first time I ever heard it.

"Nothing has changed with her."

"What's with this woman?" she asked. "There's nothing special about her. I don't get it."

My hands quickly formed fists before they relaxed. "She is special. She's the coolest, smartest, and sexiest woman I've ever known. She's my best friend. Talking shit about her isn't going to get you anywhere."

She rolled her eyes dramatically, like she was a performer on a stage. "Whatever. You want to be with her? Fine."

"I want to be with her, but I can't. But I can't keep doing this."

"What's your plan?" she demanded. "Be alone forever?"

"It's better than wasting your time." I could tell she'd already become invested in me. Her attitude stemmed from her pain. She didn't want me to leave, and she was struggling to accept it. I never should have let it get that far.

"Was I not good enough for you? Did I not satisfy you?"

That was even worse. She was finding the blame within herself. "Julia, you were amazing. Everything with you was amazing. Every time a man sees us together, he wonders what I did to land you and how he can do the same thing. If Taylor hadn't ruined me, I know things would have been different. It's not you. I promise."

She tightened her arms across her chest, pushing her tits closer together.

"I'm sorry, Julia. I really am." I didn't feel good about hurting her. I hated Derek a little bit for talking me into this to begin with. Forcing myself to have a relationship was pointless. All I did was waste my time and hers.

"Whatever," she said. "Hope you and Taylor are very happy together."

That would never happen. Sometimes when we hung out, I forgot we were just friends. We cuddled on the couch together and slept in the same bed like we were longtime lovers. I pictured taking her on my bed then making breakfast for her afterward. But those were just fantasies. I tried staying away from her, but that just made me depressed. I tried dating other women, but that just made me more depressed. I was doomed.

Fucking doomed.

"Julia, I'm sorry. I can't say that enough."

"Just go." She marched off into her bedroom and slammed the door.

I stood there for another moment and waited for her to return, just in case. When she didn't, I left.

*****

Clay's dinner sat on the table along with the textbooks and notebooks we'd be working on. My hands rested on the table, still wrapped in the gauze Taylor had placed around my knuckles.

Clay walked in right on time then fell into the chair. His eyes immediately went to my hands, and he examined the old gauze that was beginning to come loose. Minutes of silence passed, and he never said anything.

225

I waited for his usual round of questions. He would connect the dots and realize I was the one responsible for beating the shit out of his father. Instead of working on schoolwork, we'd discuss that.

Clay pulled his eyes away from my hands and looked me in the eye. The look was different than any other he'd given me. His features were blank, as if he didn't know how he should feel. His body and mind weren't in sync because everything was happening at different speeds. "Thanks…"

There was no need to clarify what he meant. "I'll always look after you."

"He's been nice to me since it happened."

"Good." He'd be stupid to do anything otherwise. "Let me know if anything changes."

He nodded then looked down at his notebook. He didn't grab his dinner or pick up his pen. He just read the passage in silence because there was nothing else to say.

And I was glad there was nothing else to say.

***

"Baby, I feel so awful about your father and I going away for the holidays. Maybe we should stay home."

"Mom, it's really fine." I spoke to her on the phone while I sat on my couch.

"But I can't leave my two babies all alone."

Connor and I never struggled with loneliness. "I won't be alone. I'm spending Thanksgiving with Taylor."

"You are?" she asked with joy. "That's wonderful. Just you two?"

My following words were going to make her erupt like a fiery volcano. "I'm going to Washington to spend the holiday with her family."

"Oh my god! That's wonderful."

I held the phone away from my ear because her voice was about to pop my eardrum.

"I'm so happy to hear that. You guys will have such a magical Thanksgiving."

"I'm sure it'll be great." I had no idea what to expect from her folks, but they must be awesome since they had an even more awesome daughter.

"I'm so happy for you. Now I just have to get Connor to settle down."

"He'll make it there on his own." I didn't know much about his personal life, but I assumed he wanted kids someday—just not right this second. "Don't worry about him."

"I feel so much better now that you have somewhere to go for Thanksgiving."

I would have been fine even if I didn't. "Have fun on your trip. Wear lots of sunscreen."

"Always. Love you, baby."

"Love you too, Mom." The second I hung up, Taylor called me. "Hey, pretty lady." It was the first thing that came to mind, and since I slipped up all the time, I didn't even bother feeling guilty about this one.

"Hey, stud. Are you home?"

"Yeah. Just got off the phone with my mom."

"What'd she say?"

"She almost had a heart attack when I told her I was spending the holiday with your family."

"I bet she did," she said with a laugh.

"So, she's happy. And that makes me happy."

"Well, I'm down the hallway. Wanted to see if I could stop by."

"The door is unlocked."

"Cool." Her voice started to echo as she came closer to my front door. "I was supposed to go on a run today, but that went to hell pretty quickly." She walked inside and shut the door behind her. When she sat on the couch beside me, she hung up.

I tossed my phone on the table. "Why did it go to hell?"

"I started stretching then lost interest. So, I ate some ice cream instead."

I chuckled. "At least you stretched."

"Yep. My muscles are so relaxed now." She pointed her toe and showed off her calf muscle. "Look at those big suckers."

"Big?" I grabbed one with my hand and gave it a squeeze. "That's all hard muscle—not big."

"Whatever." She crossed her legs and pulled away from my hand.

I actually got hard just touching her leg. I loved her legs even though she hated them. I wanted to feel them wrapped around my waist again, her ankles digging into my ass.

Change the subject.

Quick.

"So, when do we leave for Washington?"

"Wednesday. I booked our tickets."

"Where do they live?"

229

"They have a cabin in Yelm."

"A cabin?" I asked. "Like, in the mountains?"

"They live about thirty minutes outside of Mt. Rainier. It overlooks a valley of grass and faces another hill. It's beautiful. You won't understand what I mean until you see it yourself."

"Well, I'm excited. The most trees I've ever seen at once is in Central Park."

She laughed. "This place makes Central Park look pathetic."

"I look forward to the comparison. So, your folks know I'm coming?"

"Yeah, I told them I was bringing a friend."

I hated the way that word fell on my ears. I was just her friend. I hated it more and more. "Cool. So, Sage is cool with this?"

"Cool with what?" she asked.

"About you taking me to spend Thanksgiving with you and your family."

"Oh..."

So she hadn't mentioned anything.

"Shit, I forgot to tell him."

If I were lucky, this would piss him off enough that they would break up. I felt like a dick for wishing that, but I couldn't help it. I wanted it even more than I ever did before. "I don't have to go, Taylor. I don't want to mess anything up."

"No, don't worry about it. You aren't spending Thanksgiving alone."

"It's really not that bad. I don't mind."

"Nonsense. And that's final."

At least I tried to be a nice guy.

"Does Julia have plans?"

"I'm sure she does, but I have no idea what those plans might be."

She eyed me with a raised eyebrow. "What does that mean?"

"I ended it last week."

"Oh...are you okay?"

"I'm fine." *Couldn't care less, actually.*

"How did she take it?"

"She wasn't happy, but she'll get over it. I'm sure she's found another guy by now." Actually, she probably found someone the day we went our separate ways.

"Yeah, she's gorgeous."

Taylor really needed to take a look in the mirror.

"Can I ask you something?"

I wasn't sure what kind of question was directed my way, but she could ask me anything at that point. "Anything." A part of me wanted her to ask if I had feelings for her. She could initiate the conversation, so I wouldn't have to feel bad about blurting everything out.

"If you didn't really like her, why did you have a relationship with her? I thought you didn't do that sort of thing."

I wasn't sure how to answer that question without lying. "I wanted to give it a try. See if I was missing out on anything."

"And?"

It would be so much easier if I just told her the truth. I was tempted. But there would be bad repercussions. She didn't feel the same way about me, she had a boyfriend, and our friendship was on the line. I already hated not being with her, but I would hate it even more if I lost our friendship. "She wasn't the right person."

Taylor accepted that response with a nod. "You'll find her—someday."

I already did. "So...have you met Sage's family yet?"

"No," she blurted. "We aren't there yet. Not even close."

"He invited you to meet his friends."

"Yeah, but that went to shit. It really set us back."

"I thought you said everything was okay?" I didn't remember much from that night, but I do remember her coming over.

"Well...I lied."

I hung on to her every word. "What do you mean?"

"He and I got into a big fight. He was pissed I was running off to you on his birthday. I assumed we were broken up, and I'd never see him again."

Seriously? She was single? "You're available?"

"I thought I was. But he came by last week, and we worked things out. He apologized for being a jealous ass."

You've got to be fucking kidding me. I had a chance, but I was too drunk to even realize it. "Motherfucker."

"What?"

"I mean, what a motherfucker."

She shrugged. "He said he was sorry, and he was really sweet about it so all was forgiven."

Why didn't she tell me? If I'd known she was single, I would have swooped in like there was no tomorrow. "I'm glad it worked out."

"Yeah."

I leaned back into the couch and silently licked my wounds. The only good thing about the situation was they were already rocky. Could a relationship survive when it already had so many problems? There was hope, and that drove me forward.

"There's something I want to talk about."

"I'm all ears." I tilted my head toward her and stared at her lips. They were so goddamn perfect, and I wanted to suck them until they were raw. I wanted to feel her lips slide past mine as she breathed heavily into my mouth, on the verge of a climax.

"It's about Clay."

The mention of my student snapped me out of my horny funk.

"I think you should tell social services."

"I took care of it, Taylor." I made sure that piece of shit would never touch Clay again. "He even told me his father has been nice to him. I think the fear of shitting in his pants again is enough to keep his hands to himself."

"Until he gets drunk or high."

I pressed my lips tightly together and felt my jaw clench.

"I know you care about Clay, so do the right thing."

"He asked me not to. I fought him on it for a long time. I didn't make this decision lightly."

"Volt, he's a kid. He doesn't know any better."

"I can't betray him, alright? I'm all he has. This is what he wants. I'm protecting him and giving him what he wants at the same time. I admit it's not ideal, but it works."

That blue fire burned in her eyes, telling me she wasn't going to stop until she got what she wanted. "Volt, that kid deserves a better home. You need to give it to him."

"Is staying in an orphanage with hundreds of other kids really better for him?" I countered. "Will he get the attention he needs?"

"Better than being slapped around."

"It's only a year and a half. If it were longer, I'd reconsider."

She shook her head, her eyes conveying her rage.

"I see him every day, and I look after him. If something were wrong, I'd know about it. He has my number, and he knows he can call me for anything. If his dad starts drinking and things get scary, he knows I'll be there. I have his back—one hundred percent."

"But—"

"I love this kid. You really think I'd let anything happen to him?"

When I put it that way, she didn't have an argument. "Of course I know you love him. And I know you'll do anything to protect him. But I just think there's a better way."

"I think this is the way—for now."

Taylor dropped the argument when she realized it wasn't going anywhere. It was only escalating the tension between us. It felt like two parents who were disagreeing on how to raise their children. "What's your brother doing for Thanksgiving?"

"Not sure. Probably staying with a friend."

"You haven't asked him?"

"Nah." We usually only talked to each other when we were with our parents. Other than that, we kept to ourselves. Even though we lived in the same city, we never spoke to each other.

"Did something happen between you two?"

"Kinda. When we were in high school, he had a girlfriend. I slept with her."

"Oh…"

"It's more complicated than that. They broke up, and we were at a party together. She came on to me, and I was drunk, so I let it happen. I didn't think it would bother him that much but it did. We were never the same after that."

"Did you apologize?"

"Yeah. He never seemed angry with me, just indifferent."

"I think indifference is worse."

"You're right, it is. But I apologized and tried to make it right. If he doesn't want to forgive me, I can't make him. It was a long time ago, and I'm not going to keep feeling guilty about it. The ball is in his court."

She nodded in agreement. "Nobody is perfect."

"And I'm not even remotely close to being perfect."

"Maybe one day he'll let it go."

Doubtful. "Yeah."

"So, what do you want to do?"

"Strip poker?" Getting her naked was all I ever wanted to do.

She laughed it off like she thought I was joking. "How about Mario Kart?"

"You like Mario Kart?" I blurted.

"Of course. Who doesn't?"

Somehow, she made me fall harder for her. "You're on, Tayz."

"You're on, baby."

"What did you just call me?"

"Nothing...mama's boy."

Now it was on like Donkey Kong. "Don't you dare call me a mama's boy."

"Why not...mama's boy?"

I held up my hands to tickle her. "Big deal. I love my mom. So what? But you're going to pay for that anyway."

"Oh shit." She jumped up to run away from me.

I grabbed her by the waist and threw her back on the couch. I climbed on top of her and began my series of tickles, getting her right along the ribs and below the armpits. She was ticklish everywhere, so it was easy to get her good.

She laughed and tried to push me off. Her leg moved and slightly wrapped around my waist.

I pinned her arms above her head with one hand and used my free hand to get her vulnerable spots. Her eyes lit up as the sensations rocked her body. She tensed and coiled as she tried to fight off my hand.

My face was just inches from hers, and her body was pinned underneath mine. I was close enough to have her, to kiss her.

And that's all I wanted to do.

I wanted to play with her just like this, but I wanted something more. I wanted her to be mine—and mine alone. Why couldn't she feel the same way about me? Why couldn't she look at me the way I looked at her?

Why couldn't I have what I wanted?

I finally stopped tickling her and gave her some air.

She didn't pull her hands away from my grasp. She breathed hard underneath me, looking into my eyes with an open expression. Her leg was still wrapped around my ass, just the way I dreamt about.

My cards were exposed, and I was making my feelings obvious. She was a smart woman, and if I kept this up, she would see right through me. I'd already given too much away.

I cleared my throat and sat up. "I'll set up the Wii."

"Yeah…I want to be Mario."

"I want to be Bowser." I kept my back to her as I set everything up. It was a relief to hide my face—and my hard-on.

"But he's the bad guy."

I hooked up the wires and grabbed the controllers. "I'm a bad guy too."

***

Derek and I fist-bumped when we reached each other in the bar.

"What's up?" Derek asked. "Julia told me you guys broke up."

"Yeah. It didn't work out."

"How could it not work out?" he asked. "She's drop-dead gorgeous, and she was really into you."

That made me feel worse. "It wasn't going anywhere. My feelings never changed."

"Taylor has you really tight on her hook, doesn't she?"

"Yep. I'm stuck."

"So, that's it?" he asked. "You give up?"

"I'm not sure what's going to happen. I dated an amazing woman, and I still didn't feel anything. That tells

240

me I'm doomed. Maybe when Taylor gets married, I'll finally get over her."

"You think she's gonna marry that guy?"

"No. At least I hope not."

"I don't even know what to say." He ordered two beers and passed one to me. "You tried dating, you tried avoiding her…we're running out of options."

"No, we've already run out of options."

"The only thing left is fessing up."

"I'm not fessing up when she's seeing someone. That's a dick move."

He rolled his eyes. "That's not the Volt I know."

"I'm a different guy when it comes to Taylor. I'm not going to manipulate her existing relationship to get what I want. I wouldn't want her to resent me down the road. I just have to wait and hope for the best."

"Who knows how long that will be."

"Hopefully, not forever. They got into a big fight recently. That bodes well for me."

"Over what?" he asked.

"Actually…me."

"So much for not interfering."

"I didn't get involved on purpose. It just happened."

"But it still worked out pretty well."

"If they're butting heads now, they'll probably hit another bump in the road. I just hope it's soon. We were tickling each other the other day, and I almost kissed her. I'm not sure if I can control myself anymore."

"I say you should do it and see what happens."

"I'm not going to make her cheat on her boyfriend. Not cool."

"Whatever," he said. "I'd knock off the chivalry act and just take what you want. Life isn't fair, and the sooner you learn that, the better."

I wasn't against competition or doing whatever was necessary to get what I wanted. But I was against hurting Taylor. If we had a chance together, I wanted it to start on good terms. I wanted it to feel right, not tainted.

"Anyway, what are you doing for turkey day?"

"Spending it with Taylor's family." I took a drink to mask the cringe on my face.

Derek slammed his beer on the table. "Say what?"

I took a longer drink than necessary. "I figured you'd have something to say about that."

"Okay, it's official. She's got a thing for you."

"She doesn't." Even though I wished otherwise.

"Why else would she invite you to meet her damn family?"

"Because I told her I had nothing to do on Thanksgiving." It was a pity invite.

"That's still pretty ridiculous to invite you all the way to Washington."

"That's the kind of person she is," I said with a shrug. "She doesn't want anyone to be alone."

"She wouldn't have invited me."

"She probably would have, actually."

"Dude, I bet all the beer in this bar she wouldn't have invited me."

"We'll never know the answer to that so we should just let it go."

He shook his head and grabbed his beer again. "I'll never understand you two. Seriously."

I'll never understand us either.

Chapter Twelve

Taylor

I cooked dinner for the two of us, and we dined by candlelight at my kitchen table. Since I would be in Washington for nearly a week, I wanted to make the evening memorable.

I wasn't the most amazing cook in the world, but I rocked my Crock-pot like nobody's business. I made green chili chicken tacos with refried beans and rice. And it tasted pretty damn good.

"Thanks for dinner," Sage said when he finished his meal. "That was amazing."

"Thanks. I'm glad you liked it."

"Never knew you could make tacos in the Crock-pot."

"I didn't either until I found the recipe on Pinterest."

He chuckled. "Imagine what cooking was like thirty years ago when the Internet wasn't a thing. How did people find recipes?"

"A cookbook."

"Yeah, but most books are like thirty bucks. Kind of a rip-off."

"True. That's probably why frozen dinners became so popular."

He rubbed his stomach. "Ah, yes. I've had a few of those in my day."

I finished my food and felt way too full to move. I didn't want to clean the dishes in the sink, and I didn't want to clear the table. Sometimes, I wished I would wake up one morning and find out that elves broke in and took care of everything.

"So, you're flying out tomorrow?" he asked.

"Yeah. It'll be a long flight."

"How long?" he asked.

"Six hours."

"Any layovers?"

"Nope." Thank god. Long layovers made traveling a million times worse. Sitting around in a terminal with nothing to do was agonizing. And I usually felt gross after sitting on a plane.

"That's something to be grateful for. When will you be back?"

"Sunday night. Then I have work the next day."

"Brutal," he said. "At least you'll be relaxing over the holiday."

"Yeah." I knew I needed to tell him about Volt, but I kept chickening out. I wasn't even sure how to address it. Did I just blurt it out randomly? Did I bring up Volt first, and then lay it on him?

"How's Volt's student doing?"

Or he would bring him up for me. "He's still at his father's house. I told Volt to call the police, but he thinks the kid is better off where he is. We've been arguing about it."

"Why would he think the kid is better staying there?"

"Because he almost killed the dad when he jumped him in an alleyway."

Sage couldn't hide the shock on his face.

"He thinks the dad won't mess with him again. But I'm not so sure. In a few months, anything can change."

"That's some serious stuff."

"Yeah…" I had to get it over with. It was like a bandage. I just had to pull it off. "Volt's parents went on a cruise for Thanksgiving, so I invited him to spend the holiday with us." I took a drink of my margarita and acted normal, like what I said wasn't totally inappropriate.

Sage's shock immediately turned to disbelief. "Whoa, can you repeat that?"

"Volt is coming with me to Washington." I kept up my indifferent façade, but my heart was racing a million miles an hour.

"I don't remember you mentioning that." He kept his cool a lot better than last time, but his rage was building.

"I asked him that night when...he was going through a hard time." *And I thought we were broken up.*

"Don't you think that's a little weird?"

"He's my friend. Friends invite people over all the time."

"Not when they live across the country and they're dating someone else."

This was headed to a fight. I could already tell. "I know it's a little weird, but I didn't want him to be alone on Thanksgiving."

"And you're just going to tell your parents he's a friend? And nothing more?"

"I already told them that." *But I didn't mention the fact he was a dude.*

He crossed his arms over his chest, his face darkening. "I could let the kissing incident go because we were at each other's throats at the time, but this... I'm not okay with this."

"There's nothing to be okay with. Volt and I hang out all the time. We'll just be hanging out in a different state."

"With your parents," he snapped. "Spending the whole week with them while your boyfriend stays in New York. I'm sorry, but that's just fucking strange."

The F-bomb had been dropped. Shit was going down. "He's going through a hard time, and his family is out of town. I'm not going to leave him stranded."

"Why doesn't he spend the holiday with Julia?"

"They aren't together anymore." *Maybe I shouldn't have said that.*

His face started to tint.

I definitely shouldn't have said that.

He rose to his feet. "You know what? I'm not okay with this. I can get on board with you guys hanging out here and there, but I'm not cool with this. Not even a little bit."

I remained in my chair. "I'm sorry you feel that way. Again, I invited him when we were broken up."

"But we were never broken up."

"But I thought we were…"

"Well, uninvite him."

Now I rose to my feet. "I can't do that."

"Yes, you can. He'll get over it."

"No. I already told my parents I was bringing someone, and he's already packed. I'm not going to be rude and drop him like that."

"But you're going to disobey me instead?"

Whoa. Hold on. What did he just say? "Disobey?"

"Yes. You're going against my wishes."

I didn't consider myself a catty woman, but my sassiness was coming out in full force. "First of all, I don't *obey* anyone. So you better knock that off right now. I'm not someone you can boss around. Second of all, he and I are just friends, and you're turning nothing into something."

"Friends don't kiss."

"He was drunk and doesn't even remember it."

"But you weren't drunk," he snapped. "And you do remember it."

I gripped the table for balance. I was both angry and ill. This argument kept going around and around. It would never die.

"You aren't taking him with you," he said. "And that's final."

"You don't tell me what to do." I would never be okay with a man bossing me around. If he had a problem with that, he could leave. And I'd slam the door shut behind him.

"Taylor, I'm tired of this. Our relationship was perfect until Volt stepped all over it. We really hit it off, and I thought I saw this going somewhere. You have to admit your relationship with him isn't normal. It would bother any guy."

"Bother, maybe. But not turn him into an ass."

He clenched his jaw, and his hands formed fists. "This is the bottom line. Him or me."

"What?"

"Him or me," he repeated. "I feel like you have two boyfriends, and I don't like to share. So either end your friendship with him or end your relationship with me."

My entire body flinched when I heard what he said. "What? You didn't want him coming to Thanksgiving and now you want him completely out of my life?"

"Yes." His shoulders were squared like he was ready for a fight. "I'm tired of seeing him stare at you. I'm tired of calling you and hearing his voice in the background. I'm tired of him calling you when he needs a shoulder to cry on. I'm tired of sharing you. This problem is never going to go away unless he's gone. Because he's the problem. So, what's it gonna be? Him or me?"

I gripped the table and stared at the empty plates. The evening started off great and went to shit so easily. The second Volt came up, it crashed and burned.

"Him or me, Taylor?"

I liked Sage and saw a future for us somewhere down the road. Maybe we would get serious and move in together. Maybe a few years later, we would get married and have some kids. It was a future I enjoyed picturing.

But I couldn't imagine my life without Volt.

He was my best friend, the person I did everything with. Something about him comforted me. Boyfriends would come and go, but he would always be there.

I couldn't live without him. "Volt."

Sage couldn't hide the horror on his face. He looked like he'd been stabbed—right in the heart.

"I'm sorry." I really was. I didn't want to choose and it was unfair to make me. But if he drew a line in the sand, I had to cross it. "I really am."

He stepped away from the table, looking angrier than I'd ever seen him. His face was beet red, and his muscles were tense for an attack. He wanted to demolish my living room. I could see it on his face. "Hope you two are very happy together."

***

"Everything okay?" Volt sat beside me on the plane. We were sitting in coach in two seats next to a window. The constant hum of the plane was in the background, and we had to talk a little louder to hear each other. The flight attendant passed the aisle, handing out water and juice.

"Just tired." I continued to look out the window, trying to get Sage out of my head. That was the worst break up I'd ever had. The way he stormed out without looking back was enough to bring tears to my eyes.

Was I doomed to be alone forever?

I didn't expect to find Prince Charming right when I moved to the city, but I expected to have better luck than this. Sage wasn't a jerk, and I could understand his point of view, but I hated the way he went about sharing it. He was controlling and not in a good way.

I needed to talk to Sara.

She always made me feel better about break ups, threatening to kick the guys in the nuts and shave their heads. At the start of the conversation, I was usually crying, but I was always laughing by the end.

"Why don't I believe you?" He was reading a book next to me, but he shut it and tucked it into the net attached to the seat in front of him.

I didn't want to get into it right then. We were on a plane with hundreds of other people. I suspected I would start crying, and I didn't want my tears to show. Some women still looked beautiful when they cried, but I looked like an ugly ass tomato. "I don't want to talk about it right now."

Volt snaked his hand to mine under the blanket and interlocked our fingers. He didn't press me for answers as he comforted me without words. "Okay. We'll talk later."

I was grateful he let me off the hook so easily. Sara would pester me until she got exactly what she wanted. The grip of his large hand made me feel safe momentarily, even if the feeling was fleeting. Comfort in any form was appreciated.

"I wish we could play Mario Kart right now."

He made me chuckle. "Me too."

He pulled out his phone and opened a game app. "You like word puzzles?"

I nodded.

He opened the puzzle, and at the bottom of the screen was the list of words we were supposed to find. He found the first word and dragged his finger across the screen until it was highlighted with blue.

I searched the sea of letters until I found the next word. I dragged my finger across the letters until the entire word was highlighted.

"Pretty cool, huh?"

"It beats a pen and paper." I found another word and dragged my hand across the letters.

Volt stuck his finger in the way and got the rest of the letters, getting the point for finding the word.

"Hey, jerk."

His smile was anything but apologetic. "Too slow."

***

Volt was behind the wheel of the rental car as we drove from Seattle to Yelm. My house was forty-five minutes away, so it was a short drive in comparison to the flight we just endured. "Should we pick something up?"

"Like what?"

"I don't know. Pie?"

"My parents will have everything. Don't worry about it."

"So, you told them I'm a hot stud and everything? I want your mom to be prepared." He grinned at me from his side of the car.

"My mom isn't into cocky dicks, and they don't know you're a guy."

"What?" he asked. "You didn't tell them I was coming?"

"I said I was bringing a friend, and they never asked what sex you were."

"They're in for a big surprise I'm six two of all man."

"My parents aren't going to care."

"Ever brought a man around before?"

"No."

"So, I'm the first guy they'll meet?" That smile was still on his face.

"Not really. You aren't my boyfriend, so you don't count." I had a boyfriend yesterday until I got dumped. My parents would have been happy to know I was seeing someone. Now they would realize I could only get boy *friends*, not boyfriends.

"I still count," he argued.

"If you say so."

He followed the GPS until we entered Yelm. His eyes scanned the sides of the road. The lush greenery stretched for days into the distance. The trees were covered in leaves, the plump kind full of moisture and raindrops. Dirt was a rare commodity around there because grass covered every surface that wasn't asphalt. "There's so much green."

"You never get tired of it." On either side of the road were lush walkways and hiking trails.

"The air is different here. I can already tell."

"I miss it sometimes. Looking at concrete, skyscrapers, and bums gets old sometimes."

"But I bet you can't get Chinese food at three in the morning in Yelm."

"True. But I never order Chinese food anyway."

"You ever think about moving back here?"

"Sometimes," I said. "I'm not sure if New York will always be my home."

"Really?" he asked in surprise.

"Well, I don't want to raise kids in the city. I don't think it's the best environment."

"I see your point. But Washington is far away. How would you ever survive without seeing me every day?"

"You'd come with me." I smiled then checked my phone for any messages from my parents. I told them we landed and would be there soon.

Volt fell silent and didn't say anything. He drove farther from the city then headed to the hills before Mt. Rainier. It was a clear day, so the mountain could be seen in the distance, caked with white snow. "Shit, that's beautiful."

"It is, huh?"

"And that's in their backyard. Crazy."

"If we have time, I'll take you on a hike."

"You hike?" he asked.

"Hell yeah. Everyone who lives here is pretty active."

"That's cute...hiking boots with a little backpack. I can picture it."

"It's not cute," I said. "It's actually pretty exhausting. You'll see what I mean."

"I hope so."

We approached my house from a mile away. There was a turn in the road just before a view of the house. "It's going to be on the right."

"Okay."

After the bend, we could see the valley where the house was settled. It was built on the side of a hill, having a view of the greenery and the world beyond. It was secluded out there. Without the road, you'd forget other people existed entirely.

"Damn, this is where they live?"

"Yep. I grew up in that house."

"How'd they land a place like that?"

"Dad saved his money and bought the land. Then he built the house. He's a carpenter, so he built everything on his own. When he and my mom got married, she moved in."

"I understand how he landed her. Anyone would want to live in a place like that."

"I'm sure my dad had other qualities too."

"But nothing nearly as important." He nudged me in the side.

We drove up the road and entered the gate. The front of the house was covered by trees swaying high above. The dirt road was wet from the constant moisture, and the grass was greener than anything in Central Park.

"This is such a cool house."

"Wait until you see the inside of it."

We grabbed our suitcases and headed to the front door. My first instinct was to just walk inside, but I realized

I couldn't do that anymore. I hadn't lived there for five years. So I rang the doorbell.

Volt eyed the porch and the wooden chairs sitting in the corner. A table was positioned beside the sitting area. It was the place where my mom knit in the afternoons. He wore jeans and a hoodie, his powerful body obvious even in the loose fabric. He was nearly a foot taller than me, and I didn't realize how different our sizes were until then.

The front door opened, and Mom and Dad were on me quicker than I could see. Mom hugged me first and kissed me on both cheeks while Dad squeezed in and hugged me from the other side. I was being sandwiched by my folks, and I could barely breathe.

"Missed you so much, honey." Mom squeezed me again.

"I haven't been able to sleep because I've been so excited." Dad kissed my forehead just the way he used to.

"I missed you too." I pulled away from them so I could get some air. "But I need a second to breathe." I put my hands on my hips and enjoyed the air. I had a feeling I wouldn't be getting much of it during the trip.

Mom flinched when she looked at Volt. "Honey, who's this?"

"Mom, this is my friend I was telling you about. Volt."
I wished my parents would stop looking so shocked, but the
worst had already come and gone.

Still surprised, they just stared at him. They
probably couldn't believe that I brought home such a good-
looking man. Volt had the prettiest blue eyes, a stern jaw to
set them off, and he was all muscle.

"It's a pleasure to meet you." Volt shook their hands.
"I really appreciate you allowing me to spend Thanksgiving
with you. My parents decided to take a cruise to the
Caribbean. Can't say I blame them."

Mom shook his hand, but her jaw was still open. A
bug could fly in there.

Dad couldn't compose himself either. He stared at
Volt like he was a savior. "We're glad to have you. Volt, is
it?"

"Yeah," Volt answered. "It's my middle name. That's
what everyone calls me."

Mom finally snapped out of it. "We're so excited to
meet you. Thank you for coming."

"I'm very happy to be here," Volt said. "Wherever
Taylor goes, I'm not far behind."

My parents were falling in love with him. I could see it in their eyes.

"Please come in." Dad grabbed his bags and carried them inside.

No one grabbed my bags, so I did that on my own.

"Your room is just down the hall," Mom said. "Let's put your things away." They walked us down the hallway until we came to my old bedroom. There was a queen size bed and white dressers. My old teddy bear was still there.

Dad placed Volt's things on one side of the bed while Mom placed my luggage on the other side.

"Uh, Mom. Volt and I aren't sleeping together—"

"Don't be shy," Mom said. "You're a grown woman, and we understand that. We aren't going to make the two of you sleep in separate beds."

Volt turned to me, a smile on his lips. "Works for me."

"Mom, we aren't seeing each other," I argued. "We're just friends."

"It's really okay," Mom said. "There's no reason to be embarrassed."

"I'm not embarrassed," I argued. "I'm telling you, we really are just friends." My mom was so excited at the prospect of having a son-in-law that she wasn't listening. Even if she believed me, she wasn't going to let us leave unless he was my boyfriend.

"We'll let the two of you get washed up." Dad walked out and pulled Mom with him.

Mom gave us a wave before she shut the door.

This Thanksgiving had already gotten off to a bad start. "I'm sorry about that. My parents just want me to settle down and give them grandchildren."

"I don't mind." He grabbed the teddy bear and held it in his hands. "Who's this guy?"

I snatched him away and held him to my chest. "Teddy."

"That's original," he teased.

"Don't make fun of me. You were never supposed to be in here."

He walked around my room and examined the furniture and the private bathroom. "Pretty nice. I never had my own bathroom."

"Only child," I explained.

"Sounds nice."

"The grass is always greener on the other side."

He sat on the bed and felt the strength of the springs. "Your mattress is quiet... I like that." He winked.

"You aren't sleeping in here."

"Why not?" he asked. "We sleep together at home all the time."

"That's different. We're usually drunk or depressed. And I don't want my parents to get their hopes up."

"Why not? I let my parents think you're my girlfriend."

"And they're going to be devastated when they realize I'm not."

"Maybe they never have to find out."

"What?" *What did that mean?*

He tested the springs again. "You used to sneak boys in here, huh? Your parents would never hear a thing."

"I may have snuck in one or two guys..."

He waggled his eyebrows. "Bad girl... I like it."

"I was in a relationship with each of them, at the time."

"And this is where you got it on." He patted the comforter.

"You're nosey, you know that?"

"Not really. We're best friends, right?"

264

"That doesn't mean we tell each other everything."

"Actually, I'm pretty sure that's the very definition of it. So, did you lose your virginity here?"

My cheeks blushed at the question.

"There's my answer."

"Where did you lose yours?" I sat beside him with my bear in my lap.

"In the back of a truck."

"Where?"

"On the side of the road."

"What?" I blurted. That was the most unromantic thing I'd ever heard.

"I was giving a girl a ride home from a party, and one thing led to another so...I pulled over and we did it."

"How old were you?"

"Thirteen."

"Then why were you driving?"

"I borrowed my dad's truck in the middle of the night."

"Did you get grounded for that?"

He laughed. "Baby, I never get caught for anything."

I rolled my eyes.

Mom came to the closed door and knocked. "Dinner will be ready in fifteen minutes." Her feet sounded heavy as she walked away.

"Home cooked meal?" he asked. "I'm already liking it here."

"I'll move my stuff into the spare bedroom. You can have the private bathroom."

"What?" he asked. "Let's just stay together. What's the harm?"

"I already told you. I don't want my parents to think this is something when it's not."

"But they already think it. Even if you move into another room, they're still going to think it. So how about you stop fighting it and just let it go?"

***

After dinner and a game of Scrabble, we went to bed. I washed my face and brushed my teeth in the bathroom, and Volt shared the sink with me and did his nighttime ritual. He brushed his teeth and shaved before he pulled off his shirt and his jeans.

I had my own pajamas to wear even though I preferred his clothes instead. They were baggy and smelled nice. They reminded me of him throughout the night.

266

Volt got into bed first, his bare chest uncovered. He rested one hand behind his head while the other rested on his stomach. His eyes were glued to my face as he watched me get into bed.

"What?"

"Nothing." He redirected his gaze to the ceiling.

I rubbed lotion into my hands before I turned off the lamp. I got into bed and hugged my pillow, immediately thinking about Sage and how he would feel about this. Maybe he was right. He had every right to be mad. But even if that were the case, I still couldn't cut Volt out of my life. He was my crutch, my best friend, my everything. I couldn't picture my life without him—and I never wanted to.

But I was still sad.

Volt stayed on his side of the bed for a few minutes before he turned over and spooned me from behind. "So...are you ready to talk about it?"

I was hoping he'd forgotten what I said on the plane. Thinking about Sage made me sad. I wasn't sure if it was the loss of him that bummed me out or the fact my relationship with Volt really was a problem. Would any guy ever be okay with it? "Sage and I broke up."

His body remained still as he was wrapped around me. But his heart started to beat fast in his chest. I could feel it thump against me, kicking hard. His breathing accelerated as well. The breaths landed on the back of my neck, accompanying his frantically beating heart. "What happened?"

I didn't know if I should tell him the truth. It would probably make him feel bad. "It doesn't matter."

"It does matter. Tell me."

I kept my mouth shut and stared at the wall of my bedroom. My white dresser was just as pristine as the day my father built it. He used the finest wood and wax to construct it.

"It was me, wasn't it?" His voice carried his defeat, along with his sadness.

"No."

"Yes, it was," he said with a sigh. "What happened?"

"He didn't like the idea of you coming to Washington with me."

"Then you should have left me behind. I would have understood."

"But I didn't want to leave you behind. That's the problem."

He tightened his hold on me.

"Then he said I had to pick between you guys. Him or you."

"For Thanksgiving?"

"Forever."

"What?" He propped himself up on his elbow and looked down at me. "Are you serious?"

"Yeah." I turned on my back so I could look up at him.

"He actually made you choose?"

I nodded.

"And you chose me?" Surprise filled his eyes, lasting long after he finished speaking.

"Boyfriends come and go. Friends are forever."

"But…" He fell silent, his lips no longer moving. He looked around my room before he turned back to me. He remained speechless. There wasn't much he could say, so I didn't blame him for being mute.

"I'm just sad it had to end that way. I can't seem to hold a man."

"That's not the problem, Taylor. You don't put up with bullshit, and there's nothing wrong with that."

"He said some other stuff too...about me disobeying him."

"Oh damn. I bet the shit hit the ceiling then."

He knew me all too well. "I didn't want to pick him. I'll just put it that way."

He snuggled into my side and pulled me against his chest. Our faces were close to one another, and concern was written on his face. "Are you okay?"

Not really. I really liked Sage. When we met in that restaurant, I felt a tingle, the kind of sensation that overcame the body when something important just happened. It felt like the beginning of something beautiful. But it never progressed and never had a chance to grow. Invisible ropes held me back, and I was unable to pursue it head-on. But I had no idea what those ropes were. "Yeah, I'll make it through."

Chapter Thirteen

Volt

She was single.

Totally available.

And I was sharing a bed with her.

Spending the weekend with her family over the holidays was the perfect opportunity to make something happen. I could make her parents fall in love with me, and I could make her fall in love with me too.

Finally, the odds were working in my favor.

I wanted to blurt all the feelings deep inside my chest, but I knew I couldn't go straight for the kill. She just broke up with Sage, and she didn't exactly seem happy about it. If I went for it right away, I would look insensitive.

But that didn't mean I couldn't flirt with her.

Work my magic.

Make her swoon.

I got this.

We had breakfast the following morning at the dining table. Her parents asked about work and life in the city, and Taylor answered every question without showing her irritation. I knew she didn't like being bombarded with questions, and that's exactly what her parents were doing. But she was too nice to say anything.

"How did you sleep?" her father asked me.

It was strange to look him in the eye when I was obsessed with his daughter. I'd kissed her up against a wall and gotten a mini hand job from her. Awkward was an understatement. "Great. Thank you."

"Taylor has had that bed since she was a teenager," her mother said. "Who knew she would sleep in it with her... Never mind." She looked down at her porridge and took a few bites.

A storm was brewing behind Taylor's eyes.

Her parents assumed our relationship was on the marriage track. I could see them already making plans for it. But at least that meant they liked me.

"Do you guys have plans today?" her mother asked. "Are you going to show Volt Mt. Rainier?"

"If he's up for it." She turned to me, asking the question with her eyes.

"I'm up for anything, Mario."

"Alright, Bowser," she answered. "We'll see what you got."

"Mario?" her father asked. "Bowser?"

"They are Mario Kart characters," Taylor explained. "We play that game sometimes."

Her parents exchanged a look.

"Who won?" her father asked.

I groaned at the question.

"I kicked his ass," Taylor said. "He nearly cried."

"I let her win." That was a lie, but I had to save face.

"Oh, whatever," Taylor said. "You're such a sore loser."

"And you're a pompous winner," I argued.

"I've had enough of this." Taylor left the table, most of her food untouched. "Get your hiking boots."

"I didn't pack any," I answered.

"You can borrow mine," her father offered.

"Thanks," I said. "Now I'm going to humble your daughter."

"We leave in fifteen minutes." Taylor disappeared from the kitchen and walked down the hall. When her bedroom door shut, I knew she was getting ready.

"You guys are so cute together," her mother said, giving me puppy dog eyes.

"Thanks," I said. "But I think she's the one making it cute."

"Aww," her mother whispered.

"Want a tip?" her father asked. "For hiking?"

"Sure," I said. "I can't let my lady beat me too hard."

"Go at an angle," he said. "Less steep and you can move quicker that way."

"Thanks for the suggestion." I gave him a thumbs up before I left the table.

"And one more thing," her mother said.

"What's that?" I placed my plate in the sink.

"Could you take a picture together while you're up there? I want to show all my friends that my little girl has such a handsome man."

I grinned from ear-to-ear. "Why, thank you. I'll make that happen."

"Thanks so much. If I try to take a picture of you guys, she'll just throw a hissy fit," she said.

"I know what you're talking about," I said. "I'm the target of those hissy fits pretty often."

***

It was hard to keep up with her because I didn't care about the hike. Winning meant nothing to me when I was surrounded by such glorious beauty. When I looked up into the treetops, I could see the sun poking through. Drops of

274

mist constantly sprinkled down, landing on my nose and cheeks. It was lighter than a butterfly kiss.

"What are you doing?" Taylor turned around from her spot down the mountain. She put both hands on her hips and her chest rose and fell with her heavy breaths. "You're even slower than I thought you would be."

I held up my palms so I could feel the moisture coat my skin. "Does it do this often?"

"What?" She climbed back up the hill until she was close to me.

"The mist. It's not rain, and it's not snow. It's so soft."

She looked up into the sky, her hair poking out from underneath her beanie. "Yeah, it mists a lot here. People say it rains here all the time, but that's not totally accurate. Most of the time, it just does this."

"It's cool. Never seen anything like it." The mountain was lush and green with pine trees. In the background was the tallest mountain I'd ever seen, and it was covered with snow. Only bits of black rock could be seen underneath. "This is the most beautiful place I've seen."

"It's pretty great, huh?" She looked around, admiring the same view. "There's usually snow up here all year round."

"Wow."

"And it's not like the snow we get in the city. This is clean and fluffy."

"The city has nothing in common with this place."

"Let's keep going." She turned around and continued her trek down the hill.

I pulled my gaze away from the surrounding beauty and paid attention to something equally hypnotizing.

That beautiful behind.

I glanced at it from time to time as we made our way down the hill. Now that I knew she was available, I thought about her in sexual ways more than I did before. Right then, I kept picturing that ass right in my face. I'd lick her wet pussy and inhale her scent. Then I would shove myself deep inside her.

Whoa. I needed to take it down a notch.

When we reached the bottom of the trail, we encountered the river. It moved underneath the bridge swiftly, heading for the waterfall just up ahead. Snow was on either side of the bank, but it wasn't the fluffy kind on the mountain. It was covered in footprints and sludge. "Should we head back? It's getting late."

"Maybe," she said. "I'm starving."

"What's new?" I teased.

She looked back up the mountain. "I love hiking downhill. Uphill, not so much."

"I can carry you." I'd get to touch that sweet behind with my bare hands.

"I can carry myself." She walked past me and started up the trail. It was seriously steep, and it would take us a while to get to the top.

"How far is it?"

"A mile."

Damn, this was going to take a while.

She looked at me over her shoulder. "You think you can handle it?"

I stared at her ass and made it bluntly obvious what I was doing. "With a view like this, I can handle anything."

She rolled her eyes and started up the trail.

***

"Watch out," I called up ahead. "It gets muddy right here. I think it's on the left. I mean, the right."

"I don't see...shit!" Taylor slipped on the muddy bank and slid down the mountain. She tried to stop herself by grabbing a root or a bush, but she couldn't latch on to anything.

If I didn't stop her, she'd fall over the edge and plummet to her death. "I've got you. Don't worry."

She kept trying to grab a hold of the vegetation but everything slipped through her fingertips.

I hunched down and steadied my feet for the collision. Her momentum and speed were difficult to stop, but I managed to stop her with my weight. I collected her with both arms and kept her still. "See? You're fine."

"Shit, that was terrifying."

"Like I'd let anything happen to you." I stood up and grabbed her hand to help her to her feet. "It can get tricky up here. Good thing I was behind you. Otherwise, I'd have to slide down and follow you."

"Agh." She flinched and grabbed her ankle, cringing as she touched it. "My ankle… It really hurts."

My heart started to pound even though I knew she was okay. "Where?"

"I don't know… On the side."

"You might have sprained it."

"Yeah…maybe." She put her foot down but cringed again. "Stupid mud."

I eyed the trail then turned back to her. "I'll carry you."

"Are you insane?" she blurted. "Not only is it uphill, but it's a mile to the top. And the incline is about ninety percent."

"Hey, I work out."

"Thank you, Volt. But I think I can manage." She put down her foot again and tried to walk. She took one step then clenched her teeth together. She didn't make a sound, but her expression gave everything away.

"You'll make it worse if you walk on it."

"Really. I'm fine."

Damn, she was stubborn. I scooped her up into my arms and began the hike. "We can't take too long. Otherwise, we'll be here after dark. And something tells me we don't want to be here when the sun is gone."

She wrapped her arms around my neck. "I don't want you to fall and get hurt."

"Baby, you don't weigh anything. Don't even worry about it." I marched up the hill and avoided the mud she previously slipped on. Carrying her was more difficult, but it wasn't anything I couldn't handle. I'd get her to the top, safe and sound.

Besides, this was earning me some serious brownie points.

She rested her head against my chest. "Thanks for carrying me…"

"No problem."

"I should have been paying better attention. That mud was right there, and I didn't even notice."

"It could happen to anyone."

"Good thing I wasn't alone. That would have been bad."

"Let's not worry about something that never came to pass. We'll get there in one piece then take you to urgent care."

"Urgent care?" she asked in surprise.

"Yeah. We should get that ankle checked out."

"It's just a sprain. It'll go away on its own."

"Better to be safe than sorry, right?"

"But I hate going to the doctor."

"Why?" I asked.

"People are always sick. It's gross."

I chuckled. "Good to know you're so compassionate."

"I don't mean they're gross. I just don't want to get sick."

"You'll be fine. I'll take the germs before they can get to you."

"How sweet..."

Chapter Fourteen

Taylor

After an x-ray, the doctor confirmed it was a minor sprain. It would be back to normal in a few days.

A waste of a doctor's visit.

Volt drove back to the house and kept glancing at me.

"I'm fine."

"You want a painkiller?"

"It's not that bad." The swelling had already gone down, and by morning, it would be non-existent.

"There's no shame in taking some medication."

"Maybe before I go to sleep. But right now, I'm okay."

"Thanks for taking me up the mountain." He drove down the dirt road until he pulled up to the house. "It was amazing."

"Thanks for carrying me up that mountain. I hope you aren't sore tomorrow."

He put the car in park and killed the engine. "Sore? You weigh a hundred pounds. I dead-lift twice that weight every day."

I rolled my eyes and got out of the car. I tried to put weight on my bad foot, but it couldn't handle it. It throbbed in pain and made me wince.

"I've got you." He scooped me into his arms and carried me to the house.

"I can make it there on my own. I have crutches."

"Why use crutches when you have a strong man like me?" He walked into the house where my parents were sitting at the kitchen table. They were both in their pajamas and were only awake to make sure we got home okay.

"Is everything alright?" Mom stood up and eyed the clock on the coffee maker. "It's late. We tried calling, but it went straight to voicemail."

"I tripped on the hike," I explained. "Rolled my ankle."

"Are you okay, honey?" Dad asked.

"She's fine," Volt said. "We stopped by urgent care just in case, but it'll be back to normal in a few days."

Mom clutched her chest. "Oh, thank goodness."

"I'm going to get her ready for bed," Volt said. "We'll see you in the morning."

"Goodnight," I said with a wave as he carried me away.

"Goodnight," they both said.

Volt turned the corner and carried me down the hallway. He held me with ease, like I really did weigh nothing.

"Tom, I absolutely love him," Mom whispered. "I couldn't have asked for a better man to walk into our home."

"I like him too," Dad whispered. "He's a good man. And he adores Taylor."

I cringed as I listened to them, irritated they didn't believe Volt and I really were just friends. I looked at Volt's face and hoped he couldn't hear their whispers like I could.

His face didn't change as he walked into the bedroom and shut the door. "Ready for a bath?"

"I definitely need to shower. I'm so disgusting right now."

"How about a bath? Standing on one foot in the shower sounds like a bad idea."

"As long as the water is warm, I don't care." Spending all day in the freezing cold, caked in mud, brought out the girly side in me. I wanted to be squeaky clean with soft hair and glowing skin.

He set me down at the edge of the tub then started the hot water. The drain was plugged, and he added bath soap to make the bubbles grow until the bottom of the tub was obscured. "Do you think you can get undressed on your own?"

I knew I could get my shirt and jacket off, but I wasn't certain about my jeans or hiking boots. "I can give it a try."

"I have an idea." He grabbed a towel from the cabinet then placed it over my lap. He guided me to the tile floor before he proceeded to take off my shoe. He kept my ankle stabilized as he slowly pulled the boot off. He slipped it off my foot with ease.

I was expecting that to be a lot more painful.

He reached his hands underneath the towel and undid the top of my jeans. Then he slowly slid them off my hips and pulled them down my thighs. The towel covered the intimate parts of my body, but he'd already seen me in my underwear so the modesty was unnecessary.

He got the jeans to my ankles then slowly pulled them off. He was so gentle that I didn't feel even a twinge of pain. It was effortless and smooth. He tossed my jeans, shoes, and socks aside before he stood up. "Do you need help getting in the tub?"

"Ah…" No matter how I maneuvered, I would have to put pressure on my foot. And when it came to wet tile, that didn't sound like the smartest idea. "I think so."

"Hmm…" He eyed the tub then looked back at me, deep in thought. "I can just close my eyes and drop you in there."

"Close your eyes, huh?" I teased. "Like you wouldn't take a peek."

He smiled. "I might take one little peek. But I'll let you take a peek of me." He nodded toward the shower.

I felt the blood rush down south. It was hot and pounding, making my entire body light up in excitement. It came out of nowhere, and it was so powerful I wasn't sure if it was real or a byproduct of my ankle pain. "Let me take off my clothes, and then you can place me inside."

"Sounds good to me." He turned around and walked to the shower, turning on the water and getting a towel prepared. He kept his back to me the entire time. "Let me know when you're ready."

I stripped everything off and remained on the floor, freezing now that nothing was covering me. I crossed my arms over my chest and pressed my knees tightly together to fight off the cold. "I'm ready. And please hurry. My ass is frozen."

He turned around and walked toward me, his eyes shut. He felt the edge of the tub first before he kneeled beside me.

"I know your eyes are cracked."

The grin returned. "They're really not."

"Uh-huh."

"If a lady doesn't want me to see her naked, I don't see her naked. It's that simple." He touched my knees before he slid his arm underneath. His other arm went to my back. "Ready for this?"

"Yeah." I hooked my arms around his neck.

He lifted me into the air then gently set me into the water. "Is it too hot?"

"No."

He set me farther inside until my body touched the bottom. The warm water enveloped me, and I finally felt comfortable after hiking in the snow all day. My ankle felt better too.

He pulled his arms back and let them drip over the tub. His eyes were still closed. "Comfy?"

"Yeah." I fixed the bubbles across my body so he couldn't see anything. "You can open your eyes now."

His eyes opened, and he immediately looked at where my tits would be. "Dang. I was hoping that was an invitation."

"Sorry. But you aren't missing anything anyway. I'm flat as a board."

"Are not," he said with a sarcastic laugh. "And yes, I've looked."

"But I don't have the boobage Julia had."

"Whatever," he said. "Women come in different shapes and sizes. Bigger isn't necessarily better."

"Said no one ever."

He chuckled. "Believe me, you've got all the right curves in all the right places." He grabbed a towel and rolled it up before he placed it underneath my head as a pillow. "You need anything? I'm going to hop in the shower."

"You're going to shower right in front of me?" The shower was made entirely of glass. I could see every little thing—or every big thing.

"I'll hang a towel on the rack on the door. You won't be able to see the good stuff. Of course...unless you want to." He winked then walked back into the bedroom.

Now I couldn't get that image out of my head.

He came back with a towel wrapped around his waist. A towel was already hanging from the door, so he stepped inside, undid the towel, and then tossed it over the wall and onto the floor. The towel on the door blocked my sight of his manhood, but I could see everything else.

The water ran down his hair and immediately soaked it. It fell toward his face, and he ran his fingers through it to pull it back. His shoulders were meticulously carved from the muscle underneath his skin. Each individual muscle was highlighted as if chiseled from stone. The shoulder was the most vulnerable area and easy to injure, but his body looked impenetrable.

He squirted shampoo into his hand and massaged it into his hair. The soap foamed and leaked down his face, forcing him to close his eyes. He scrubbed his scalp and the back of his neck, the soap trailing down his chest and arms. His pecs were hard and muscular, reminding me of concrete. The image of his body stopped just below his belly button, and I found myself stewing in disappointment that it didn't go any farther.

Oh my lord, he was hot.

Volt rinsed the shampoo out of his hair then looked at me through the glass. "Like what you see?"

"Uh, no." I quickly turned away and pretended not to stare. "I thought I saw a spider."

"Yeah, sure," he said with a chuckle.

I looked at my toes as they peeked above the bubbles. They were bright blue because I just painted them the other day. I kept my body below water so he couldn't see anything, and I was grateful he couldn't. I suspected my nipples were pointed and hard, and the area between my legs was turning a deep shade of pink.

"You know what?" Volt said as he rubbed soap into his chest. "We can tell people we bathed together. It's true—technically."

"I'm not telling anyone that." Now I couldn't deny Sage's words. This really was weird. Volt and I had a relationship that only the best of friends had. I would do this with Sara, but that was different. The fact he was an attractive man, and I was a woman, made this beyond inappropriate. Maybe Sage was right. Maybe I was wrong.

He rinsed the soap from his body then killed the water. "I feel so much better now. I'm not used to mud and dirt."

"Just pollution and bums."

"Yeah." He chuckled then cracked the door open so he could snatch the towel. He quickly tied it around his waist, hiding all the goodies from view.

I needed to stop staring.

He stepped out of the shower and grabbed the other towel off the floor. He ran it through his hair and gave it a quick dry before he tossed it on the counter. Then he walked to the counter and shaved his face.

I remained absolutely still, suddenly aware of how naked he was. Just a simple towel was wrapped around his waist. And I was completely naked under the water. I felt like a married couple getting ready for bed.

This wasn't normal.

He washed his face and brushed his teeth. Once he was finished, he walked back into the bedroom. "I'm not coming back, so you can do whatever you need to do."

"What's that supposed to mean?" I blurted. He thought I was going to touch myself or something?

He paused at the doorway. "Wash your hair...scrub yourself. What did you think I meant?"

My face suddenly went pale despite how warm I was. "Nothing..."

He gave me a curious look before he walked out and shut the door behind him.

When I was alone, I was finally able to relax.

But the area between my legs wouldn't stop throbbing.

***

Volt and my dad went on a hike through the valley. My dad didn't use trails when he went out into the wild. He just relied on his compass and the sun to figure out where he was going. Volt immediately jumped on the opportunity, loving the chance to be outdoors.

I stayed home with Mom because I couldn't walk. My foot was better, but it still wasn't back to normal. It probably wouldn't bear my weight until we returned to New York.

Mom knitted in the rocking chair while I lay on the couch, my foot propped up and elevated. The TV was on, and *I Love Lucy* played. I used to watch it all the time when I stayed home from school on a sick day.

"So…Volt seems to be a fine young man." Mom kept her eyes focused on her knitting even though she just started a conversation that wouldn't end well.

"He is," I answered. "But he's not my boyfriend."

"Is he gay?"

"No," I blurted.

"Are you?"

"Mom!"

"If you aren't gay and you're sleeping together, he's your boyfriend."

"Mom, we really are just friends. Best friends."

"Who are in love with each other."

Mom was so determined to see me married and pregnant that she would see things that weren't really there. "Mom, I admit it's a little strange. Okay, it's really strange. But I'm telling you the truth."

"A man doesn't fly across the country to meet a woman's parents if he's just looking for friendship. I see the way he looks at you. It's exactly the way your father looks at me."

It was a sweet thing to say, but completely inaccurate. "Volt doesn't have feelings for me. Trust me on that."

She set down her knitting supplies and gave me a hard look. A lecture was coming. "I thought you were smart and perceptive."

"I am."

"You seem pretty blind to me."

"Ouch…"

"Sorry, honey. But it's true. This man loves you. I can see it written all over his face every time he looks at you. Maybe he's not your boyfriend now, but he's not going to stop until he is."

It was so ridiculous I wanted to laugh. "Whatever." I wasn't going to fight it anymore. If it made her happy, then I didn't really care.

"Don't *whatever* me." She pointed a finger at me. "I'm your mother, and I know best."

Yeah, okay. "Mom, I had a boyfriend until the other day…when he dumped me."

Her sassiness died down when she heard what I said. "What boyfriend?"

"His name was Sage. We saw each other for a few months, but we kept fighting over Volt."

"Why Volt?"

"Sage was always jealous of him. When I invited Volt to spend Thanksgiving with us, he got upset. He gave me an ultimatum. I had to cut Volt out of my life or lose him as my boyfriend."

Mom gave me a sad look. "And you chose Volt."

"He's my best friend." I felt defensive about the subject. I shouldn't have needed to explain why I threw away a good relationship for a friend. "I can't picture my life without him. I want a boyfriend that can be friends with Volt too. I want both."

"I don't think there's anything wrong with that."

At least someone agreed with me.

"But I also think Sage had a point. How would you feel if your boyfriend hung out with some woman all the time?"

I probably wouldn't like it. "I see what you mean."

"So maybe his request wasn't too radical."

Maybe not.

"And maybe the best way to avoid it again in the future is to...be with Volt."

She went for the kill—again. "Mom, it's not like that."

"Why not?" she demanded. "Are you telling me that you're really not attracted to that man? Because he's the biggest piece of eye candy I've ever seen."

I couldn't hold back the laugh. "Mom…"

"You aren't attracted to him?"

"Well…" I remembered our recent kiss with vivid detail. That kiss was hypnotic, amazing. I felt my entire burn in a way it never did for anyone else. It was just lust, but it was powerful. "Yes."

"And he's your best friend so you're more than compatible. So, what's the hold up?"

"When we first met, I was into him. I couldn't stop thinking about him and wanted him to ask me out. But then I realized he was a typical player, a man blowing in the wind and sowing his seeds. He said he never wants to settle down. So, I settled for being his friend."

"And that's the only reason?"

"Not really. After that, we became good friends. I stopped looking at him like that. I started seeing other guys and didn't see him that way anymore."

"And what about now?" she asked.

"Well...we had this kiss the other day. He was drunk and doesn't remember it, but I do. I definitely felt something."

"Then why don't you go for it?" Mom always saw things in black and white. Nothing was too complicated.

"Because nothing has changed. Volt isn't a one-woman type of guy. I'm not looking for a one-night stand. I'm looking for a forever."

"And I think he can give that to you."

I wanted to roll my eyes. "Volt is a gentleman around you guys, but he's not so clean cut all the time. I know him better than you do."

"Maybe," she said. "But you're also biased from months of knowing him. I'm seeing him right now, in this moment, and I'm telling you what I see. And that man is in love with you."

Mom thought everyone was in love with me. She thought I was the prettiest and smartest girl in the whole world. That's what moms do.

My phone started to ring, and I saw Sara's name on the screen. "Sorry, Mom. I've got to take this. I told Sara I would call her back yesterday but totally forgot."

"It's fine." She returned to her knitting. "Give her my love."

"I will." I walked into the bedroom I shared with Volt and took the call.

"Hey," she said into the phone. "Long time, no talk."

"Sorry I forgot to call you back."

"That's a big no-no. It's against best friend law."

"I'm sorry I broke the code." My sprained ankle screwed up my entire day. And sleeping next to Volt when I couldn't stop picturing him naked didn't help. I hardly got any sleep last night.

"How's your Thanksgiving?"

"Good. Yours?"

"I'm stuck in New York, so it's pretty crappy."

"But I bet it's quiet."

"Yeah, not as many people. But on Black Friday, it's gonna get cray cray," she said. "What's new with you?"

"Nothing. Volt went hiking with my dad, and I stayed home."

"Whoa, hold on. You brought Volt?"

"He had nowhere to go for Thanksgiving."

"And Sage was totally cool with it?"

"Sage was...not exactly happy. We broke up, actually."

"What?" she blurted. "Are you serious?"

"Yeah..." *Not a great way to start the holidays.*

"Are you okay?"

"I'm fine. A little bummed out but fine."

"What happened?"

I was tired of telling this story because I said it so many times. "Basically, he doesn't like Volt spending so much time with me so he made me choose between them."

"And you chose Volt."

"He's my best friend. What was I supposed to do?"

"Not choose him," she said simply. "Come on, your relationship is strange as hell. If I had a man, I wouldn't want him up in some other girl's business."

"But it's not like that."

"I don't know if I believe that..."

Not her too. "I'm not lying. I don't have feelings for Volt. He and I would never work out. He's too superficial and flakey. He tried being in a relationship with some woman, but that only lasted a few weeks until he got bored with her. And I'm telling you, this woman was drop-dead gorgeous. If he can't make it work with her, then he's a terminal bachelor. Plain and simple."

"Then why did you sacrifice a good relationship for him?"

"I sacrificed it for our friendship, nothing else."

"Sage was hot. You showed me pictures of him."

"I know. Sage was the perfect guy."

"Then make it right, Taylor. It's not too late."

"I don't know. I can't live without him."

"Who? Sage or Volt?" she asked. "Wait, it's Volt, isn't it?" Disapproval was in her voice.

"Yes..."

"Man, that's messed up."

"I know. But I can't explain it. When I'm with him, he makes me feel...like I can do anything. He always has my back and makes me feel important. He makes me laugh, makes me smile. He's gotten me through some tough times, and I trust him. He wouldn't lie to me, and that's something so rare to find. If I had to be locked in a room with someone for a week straight, he would be my first choice."

"Thanks..."

"I'm just saying."

"It sounds like any boyfriend you ever have will always be second place."

"Isn't that how it should be? Your friends before your lovers?"

"Yeah...until you get married. And then it switches."

"Well, I'll need a man secure enough to put up with it."

She laughed into the phone. "Good luck with that. No guy's going to want some dog sniffing around his woman."

"I can assure you there's no sniffing going on." The door creaked and then it clicked when it shut against the panel. I was lying on my stomach on the bed so I glanced over my shoulder to see who was there.

But there was no one.

"Taylor?"

"Hmm?"

"Where did you go?" Sara asked.

"I thought someone came inside, but I guess I'm hearing things. Anyway, are you seeing anyone?"

Chapter Fifteen

Volt

I can't live without him.

He makes me laugh, makes me smile.

If I had to be locked in a room with someone, he's the first person I would choose.

I had no idea she felt that way about Sage. I assumed he was some guy she was casually seeing. From the way she talked about him, it was like she loved him. Maybe she didn't tell me the truth because she didn't want to hurt my feelings—to let me think I was the reason she lost him.

I walked back into the kitchen and felt my mind swirl in a whirlwind of information. Taylor was talking to someone on the phone, probably Natalie, and I heard a conversation that was none of my business.

I'm pretty sure she didn't notice I was there.

"You alright, honey?" Taylor's mom set her knitting stuff on the counter before she walked up to me.

"Oh, I'm fine." I shook off the despair that ransacked my heart. "Just need some water before I hop in the shower."

"Allow me." She grabbed a cup and filled it with ice before she hit the pad on the fridge and filled it with water. "Had a good day today?"

I kept thinking about Taylor. She spilled her heart out, saying how much she missed Sage. She seemed sad on the plane and when we were in bed together, but I didn't realize just how down she was. "It was beautiful. Your husband is quick on his feet."

"He's definitely an outdoorsman."

"I'll say." I downed the entire glass of water before I set it in the sink.

"Volt, can I ask you something?"

"Of course." I turned back to her, trying to seem calm and rational. My mind was going haywire with everything I heard, and it wouldn't slow down.

She crossed her arms over her chest and examined my face like she would find the answer there. "You love my daughter, don't you?"

I assumed she was going to ask me to take out the garbage or help her with something around the house. A point blank question like that shattered my brain. I couldn't even keep a straight face.

"Because you should tell her. Everyone sees it except her." She gave me a smile before she drifted away. She grabbed her knitting supplies off the counter and returned to the living room. *I Love Lucy* playing on the TV screen.

Stunned, I just stood there.

***

Our plane was about to touch down in New York, and I was eager to be home. I had a lot on my mind, and I needed space to sort everything out. My relationship with Taylor wasn't what I thought it was. She was the animal, and I was the tick. I was sucking her dry until nothing was left. I was the reason she was unhappy.

I was the reason for her despair.

"Volt?"

"Hmm?" I turned to her and tried to desensitize myself to her beautiful face. No matter how many times I looked at it, I fell harder. Her eyes were a little brighter, her lips a little fuller. Every detail of her face was exquisite, and my eyes drank her in like drops of rain in a desert.

"Everything alright? You've been quiet for the past few days."

I didn't know how to act anymore. I kept a void of distance between us, a gaping hole bigger than a crater.

Anytime she got close to me, I hurt her. "I think I got a bug. Haven't felt like myself lately."

"I haven't heard you cough or sneeze."

"I'm good at holding it in. You know, since you hate sick people." Keeping it light was the best tactic.

"Can I get you anything?"

"No, I'm good. I have a lot of work to catch up on at the office. I'll probably be busy for a while." And I wouldn't take any of her phone calls or return them.

"Well, I hope you had fun in Washington. It was nice to be home."

"I had a great time." *Until I realized how big of an ass I was.* "Thanks for bringing me along."

"Thanks for coming."

The plane finally landed and taxied to the terminal. I couldn't wait to get off the damn thing and get out of there. The longer I was with her, the more difficult it became to be near her. I was poison to her, and she didn't even realize it.

"Are you sure you're alright?" She examined me with her smart eyes, catching something I kept trying to hide.

"Absolutely."

***

As much as I hated this, I had to do it.

There was no other way.

Taylor was miserable because of me.

And I had to make it right.

I ruined whatever chance I might have had with her, and I probably would never get the opportunity to be with her again.

But that was how it had to be.

I had to say goodbye to her.

And our friendship.

Sage opened the front door and didn't hide his surprise when he saw me. He narrowed his eyes, suspicious. He kept one hand on the door so he could slam it if necessary.

"Busy?"

"Depends."

"I want to talk about Taylor."

The mention of her name made him more irritated. "Had a good holiday?"

I deserved the jab. I knew it. "Give me five minutes."

"Fine. Go." He didn't invite me inside, keeping his body in the way.

"Give Taylor another chance. Please."

His formidable expression never changed. "She made her choice. She picked you."

"But she didn't want to."

"No. She made it pretty damn clear."

I wasn't walking away until I got what I wanted—what Taylor wanted. "I understand why you're threatened by me. I'm always around and—"

"You're obsessed with her. You're hung up on her. You date beautiful women in an attempt to forget her."

Damn, he was good.

"I'm not the jealous type, but I can't handle that."

"I agree," I said. "So, I'll disappear."

Not understanding what I meant, he cocked an eyebrow. "What?"

"I'll go away. I'll ignore her and dodge her left and right until she forgets about me."

He crossed his arms over his chest. "Why would you do that?"

"Because she misses you. Because she can't live without you. Because she wants this to work."

He didn't believe a word I said. "Where are you getting this from?"

"I heard her say it."

"To you?"

"To a girlfriend on the phone."

He shook his head slightly. "She must have been talking about someone else—probably you."

"I heard her say your name." There was no mistaking it. "Please give her another chance. I'm bowing out. You can have her."

"At least you admit it," he said darkly. "I've been telling her that for months, but she never believed me."

"She sees what she wants to see."

He leaned against the door, his poker face still on.

"I'm out of the picture now. She's yours."

He rubbed the back of his neck and looked at the ground.

I patiently waited for an answer.

When our eyes met, he wore a look of resignation. "No. She's not."

"I give you my word I'll back off. You won't see me again."

"No, she's not mine," he said. "She was never mine."

"Not true, man."

"I believe you. I'm sure you would make good on your word and leave us alone. But that's not the problem."

"Then what is?"

He chuckled under his breath. "You don't get it."

"Get what?" I asked in frustration. "I'm giving you what you want."

"But I'm not what she wants. You are."

The blood drained from my face. I could feel it leave my lips.

"She can deny it all she wants, but I know you're the man she wants. You're the one she's in love with. You're the man she can't live without—not me. Despite how much I like her, I can't be with a woman when I know she prefers someone else over me. I can't compete with you. Even if you disappear, you'll never really be gone. Because she'll never forget about you. So, I'm done. I'm the one bowing out."

Nothing he said was true. "I heard what she said—"

"You heard her wrong." He crossed his arms over his chest. "She and I will never work out. It's a nice gesture to try, but it's a waste of time."

As much as I wanted to believe what he said, I couldn't. It was too good to be true.

"The ball is in your court, man. Because I'm never going to change my mind."

I failed. I didn't fix all the damage I caused. Now Taylor would be sad for months.

"Volt, I really mean this..."

I looked up at him, unsure what he was going to say.

"You two are meant for each other. And I hope you get her."

The story continues in *Burn*, Book 3 of the Electric Series.

Available Now.

Dear Reader,

Thank you for reading Spark. I hope you enjoyed reading it as much as I enjoyed writing it. If you could leave a short review, it would help me so much! Those reviews are the best kind of support you can give an author. Thank you!

Wishing you love,

E. L. Todd

Want To Stalk Me?

Subscribe to my newsletter for updates on new releases, giveaways, and for my comical monthly newsletter. You'll get all the dirt you need to know. Sign up today.

www.eltoddbooks.com

Facebook:

https://www.facebook.com/ELTodd42

Twitter:

@E_L_Todd

Now you have no reason not to stalk me. You better get on that.

EL's Elites

I know I'm lucky enough to have super fans, you know, the kind that would dive off a cliff for you. They have my back through and through. They love my books, and they love spreading the word. Their biggest goal is to see me on the New York Times bestsellers list, and they'll stop at nothing to make it happen. While it's a lot of work, it's also a lot of fun. What better way to make friendships than to connect with people who love the same thing you do?

Are you one of these super fans?

If so, send a request to join the Facebook group. It's closed, so you'll have a hard time finding it without the link. Here it is:

https://www.facebook.com/groups/1192326920784373

Hope to see you there, ELITE!

41529985R00178

Made in the USA
Middletown, DE
16 March 2017